Praise for
Not Quite a Disaster After All

Buku Sarkar knows intimately the worlds she paints with strokes of startling beauty and pain. Her men and women—and especially her children, and the haunting secrets they carry—will remain with readers for a long time.

—**Chitra Banerjee Divakaruni**
author of *The Last Queen* and *Independence*

Not Quite a Disaster After All is sparkling debut, acutely observed and stylishly rendered, about intimacy and its aftertaste. It's also quietly, languidly funny.

—**Mohammed Hanif**
author of *A Case of Exploding Mangoes*

Each sentence in this book shimmers with a quiet luminescence. These are stories of people divided between places, old selves in new worlds. With the poetry of Sandra Cisneros and the simplicity of Jhumpa Lahiri, Buku Sarkar weaves a book about homes lost and homes we yearn.

—**Bilal Tanweer**
author of *The Scatter Here is Too Great*

Sarkar's stories are smart, kind, attentive to detail, populated with people you want to spend time with and learn more about. A major accomplishment.

—**Aleksandar Hemon**

Not Quite a Disaster After All

FLOWERSONG
PRESS

poetry by
Buku Sarkar

FlowerSong Press
Copyright © 2025 by Buku Sarkar
ISBN: 978-1-963245-40-0

Published by FlowerSong Press
in the United States of America.
www.flowersongpress.com

Set in Adobe Garamond Pro

NOTICE: SCHOOLS AND BUSINESSES
FlowerSong Press offers copies of this book at quantity discount with
bulk purchase for educational, business, or sales promotional use. For
information, please email the Publisher at info@flowersongpress.com.

*For my
only twin.*

table of contents

Not Quite a Disaster After All

I.

AFTERNOONS

Of all the compartments of day that passed through that house, the hours I remember most vividly were of the afternoon. When time moved slowest of all, dragging away with it, all the hysteria from the morning. It was when the sun moved from shutter to shutter, past furniture and bed spreads, over tapestries and rugs and across stone floors, polished doors and brass knobs, room through room, onto the walls on the opposite side of the house. In the safety of the afternoon, nothing happened. Nothing was expected. There was no school, no chores, no aunts or uncles or cousins to endure. In this house filled with voices and footsteps, a time allowed and a time needed to bridge the discrepancy between who you were and who you wanted to become.

Under the canopy of the day, you could see, from this distance, how shattered the world was that we lived in and how beautiful its dust.

But from memory, all the people in our house chased the afternoons away—with naps and televisions and the chill of the air conditioner.

The women in the house would retire—each to their own chamber, on their respective floors—after having tended to the children, to the kitchen and the prayer room. It was when their real lives began—behind closed doors, in darkness, breathing into their grief.

My grandmother, in a mound of white, in her small day room on the first—resting before once again bellowing out her life's losses in a high-pitched rage.

My eldest aunt in her room, a floor above, having taken care of everyone's lunch, pleased that the cake she had toiled over all morning had turned out well. There was always a cake cooling on the black coffee table outside. She had the air conditioning on even during the day. I can picture her angelic nose, the lips, pointing up towards the ceiling as a stillness, even calmer than her normal demeanor, took over. I imagine she was thinking about her two children—fussing over their meals in her sleep, their clothes, their school chores. When she'd awake from her nap, she would ask for tea and then her busy footsteps would sprawl against the green stone. Her smile so balanced you'd never know uncle came home in another stupor the previous night and had sat on top of the mosquito net, his heavy frame making the bed poles lean inwards, on top of her sleeping body.

My second aunt, a new addition to our family, in her own room—by the staircase and the little kitchenette on the second floor—watching a Hindi film in her room, the television set kept high on top of a cabinet so she could see it from her king sized bed. Her room still smelling of the discontent of whisky and cigarettes even though my other uncle had long gone to work.

And outside, in the living room where truth was knocking—a handkerchief fallen from someone's waist, a cup with pink lipstick marks. Ruins of their sadness.

My mother like my father and his brothers were at work. G had made sure the windows were closed three-quarters of the way to keep the sun out. He had switched off fans in rooms not being used. And then he too would curl inside the patience of the day, in his quarters in the outhouse. I wandered through the silence and the dreams, through the terrace, free and unnoticed. Afternoons were bleak, without the promises of a new day like nightfall, but afternoons were a time to imagine—of all the things that would never be true.

I'd never been at home in that house—even at the age of five. I would look at the green stone floors with the yellow borders that cascaded down like a royal carpet, and know, intrinsically, somewhere inside that something was missing in my life.

I never knew what that 'thing' was—other than knowing that I didn't have it. I would search for it all afternoon—walking from one dark and empty room to another. Touching bedsheets and windows. I would open closet doors and look inside. There was not a crack in the house that wasn't filled with things—cabinets full of food, antique furniture, carved divans in shining mahogany, chandeliers and statues and glass cases in my grandmother's room filled with all the mementos she had collected during her travels across the world. A flamenco dancer, dressed in white and pink lace, her arms moveable and also easily breakable, was my favorite. In my own room, I had a collection of dolls that my father would bring back from

London, a small electronic synthesizer I would occasionally pour my laments into. But nowhere, could I find what I was really looking for. Somewhere out there was my real life—hidden beneath folds of bliss.

It was only when my parents took me abroad for the first time that summer, instead of leaving me with the larger family, did I get a glimpse of it. Amongst various places in Europe and many museums with large paintings, we went to a small town near Zurich, where we stayed in an old converted palace by the lake. I liked this town the best as it was devoid of any historic monuments and sights and there were only two directions to go: to the left of the hotel, which lead into a corridor of trees, bordered by the lake on one side and on the other—green that went on past endlessness. If one walked along the pebbled path long enough, one came across a small playground with two swings made of tire, and a climbing wall made of blue nylon rope. The path to the right of the hotel led to the center of town and to the old wooden bridge you had to cross in order to get to the small spray of shops. There was a jewelry shop right in the corner before you turned into the puzzle of lanes.

One evening, on a walk to town with both my parents, for a little 'window shopping' as my mother called it while my father winked at me—indicating, in silence, that the chocolate shop would well be on the way—I saw a boy and a girl. Much older than me to call them children but still too full of mirth to call them adults. They were walking up front. It was chilly although the sun was out and they strolled wrapped together, their hands in each other's back pockets. The girl was wearing jeans and a short jacket that ended at her waist. Her long, wavy hair blew freely in the whispering wind. They walked slowly, stopping every once in a while, at which point we overtook them, and then continued past us as my father paused to take photographs of my mother in front of the lake. My father was a perfectionist, which meant that these pauses were long enough for them to make quite a headway and I'd find myself constantly looking over, so as to not lose sight.

The boy and the girl didn't seem to be going anywhere particular and with no urgency—the way my father always walked. Instead, they loitered on the promenade, moving as slowly as the lake, their legs crossing lazily in front of each other, unperplexed by the world around them. They looked towards each other and kissed. There were only three people there on that busy promenade—the girl, the boy and the splintering lake.

That moment, which I remember so vividly, was what I was fundamentally missing. Not a boy or a kiss, neither of which I had seen in our house, but the space to behave and be, without any judgement, without any care as to who was nearby. It was not defiance. It was freedom.

I was her in another life.

I could have been her.

Can you miss someone you've never known?

When we returned from the trip, my days felt pointless and incomplete and often I would walk around the mid-day house with a hollow feeling in my chest, searching for something, that moment.

It was on one such day, while moving through the patience of the afternoon with no real purpose, I was startled to find G still upstairs, making sure each shutter was closed. The rains would come soon.

G was one of the fourteen workers in the house. Aside from him, there were the other cleaners, the cook, the gardener, the drivers and the guards who came on rotation. I didn't know all their names. I didn't know our Bhramhin cook and I can't visualize his face although he would be present few feet away from me, separated by a wall, at every meal. He rarely left the kitchen except for the afternoons and later, after dinner was served. Nothing is lonelier than being surrounded by nameless faces.

G did the dusting and sweeping upstairs, on our floor. He was lucky enough to escape the duties of the first, which would mean working under my grandmother's wing—a curse that fell on another poor man whose name I didn't know, although I would hear my grandmother shouting at him through the open windows and dirty white grills of her verandah often enough.

G was the youngest worker in our house. I don't know if he had just finished school or was married with children but I never felt at ease around him the way I did with A—who was also bequeathed with the duties of dusting and cleaning upstairs. There was something deferential and fatherly in A's face, marked by time—the pockmarks, the leathered skin— that I trusted. Perhaps this distrust of G had to do not so much with his age but with the fact that I once saw him whipping the dog with her chain while taking her to the terrace, where she was given a weekly bath.

G saw me and stopped in his tracks. He came closer to the square coffee table and leaned forwards on it. He banged his feet against the floor, making an attempt to jump. The sun, through an open shutter burned across one side of his face making his features indistinguishable in its embers. I didn't normally play with G but he was always there, upstairs, and invariably joined our games in the terrace or sometimes in-between cleaning.

That afternoon, thankful for the aversion and company, no matter how fleeting, and not wanting to be in the mud of my own thoughts any longer—I ran to one side of

the table as he chased me from the other. Squealing, I circled the table till it became evident it would not provide for adequate buffer. I headed in small puddled steps into my parents room and threw myself backwards onto the cream spread of what was their wedding bed. My parents room adjoined mine and together formed the Master Suite of the house. I wandered into that room often when no one was around—inhaling the many scents of forbiddances. A room I let go in readily, all the masks I wore through the day.

G followed behind me. "Got you," he said and grabbed my stick like legs as he lunged, knee forwards onto the floor.

The bedroom was still cool from the previous night's air conditioning and spots of mist speckled my skin. The smell of my mother drifted in from the small dressing area, which was next to the door. It was an area I was not allowed to enter—my mother fiercely guarding the flimsy wisps of her many elaborate wigs, which she knew I so coveted.

G's large hand held both my ankles in one grip. His palm was honey colored and rough with not a single blemish. When I think of G's skin, I think of a smoothly poured chocolate ganache. His hair, cut in a mullet like shape stood erect, and gave him extra height. He was dressed in white cotton pants and white cotton button down top, with one breast pocket to the left, as all the workers in the house were.

Something about G was slimy and dirty, even though his face was spotless. It was his smile—too easy, too self-satisfied.

I wasn't wearing shoes and he tickled my feet. I squirmed and laughed more than was necessary in order to encourage him to continue. He tickled my shin and then my knees and gradually it wasn't tickling anymore but a light, gentle brush with his hand.

It continued upward and towards my thighs, stopping and playing at the border where my dress touched my skin. I didn't move. I knew something more was meant to happen then and my body, although stiff, wanted to find out.

These intermissions of the day—how devastating it's gnawing calm and how beautiful, its unsayable melancholy.

I could sense the pressure of G's grip and his touch, even though light. What I felt was no longer a tickle—pleasant yet dangerous—which, like my loneliness, I couldn't describe. But while my loneliness was entrenched in the absence of something, this was real—something airy, something feathery, yet compressed with things I understood in a heartbeat.

My hair stood at its end and my legs and arms felt cold. G looked at me from his kneeling position. His starving eyes were white. He wasn't smiling but his nostrils flared as he breathed heavily while clumsy air slid out from my mouth. I couldn't keep looking at his face and glowing eyes so I closed mine. I let his hand continue till it reached past the edge of my skirt and moved into my groin. They were trembling. His fingers long and taking their time—slippery, crawling. Everything shaking, everything blurry.

I sat up with a start and looked towards the door to see if anyone was coming. The afternoon had come to a stop. Beads of sweat on G's nose, his eyes still holding me firmly in place, as though daring me to play on in this game. I wanted to continue, I wanted his hands to keep stroking me, to feel the spreading coolness not just in my legs but my stomach and my arms. Something stopped me from moving—not just from running away, which I could have easily done, but also of continuing any longer. It was a smell coming from his clothes—of oil and onions—odors that stick to dirty kitchens and garbage bins.

A chilling alertness rose in me—to the fact that I was not meant to feel this way.

His hand climbed higher and I felt the warmth of his skin and it was then that I really knew, like the kiss by the lake, that this was wrong.

To want.

These were the rules that I had been born with.

I couldn't describe it before, this thing I had been looking for, but I understood it—the privilege of the lake, the line that had been crossed today—and I understood that this knowing could only take place within the sigh of an afternoon, secret and heavy—as solitude was.

From the corner of my eyes, I could see G's shirt was yellowing, like stale vegetables. I tried to hold my breath.

I wasn't afraid, although I didn't feel safe. There was nothing safe about freedom, about coming out of hiding from inside yourself.

No one out there can save you.

I giggled one last time and ducking under his arm, skipped out of the room as though we were in just another chase. I turned the corner of the living area, now under the covers of early evening and into the soft light of my cousins' chambers. G didn't follow although I could still hear his breath between my legs.

There my two little cousins were, the girl asleep on her bed while her brother played with bricks. The air conditioner was on and the bed covers tussled. Through the slits of the plastic blinds, a sickly light fell in, making the room look like a hospital.

I skid onto the cool floor next to him. "Let's build a hotel," I said. The stone of the floor teased my insides, which were still cold and full of fire from moments before.

My cousin, although a year older, dutifully gathered up the pieces and we went on to build a magnificent four-storied structure—with white windows and green shutters, a green tiled roof and pink flowers on the window ledges.

Soon, the sky changed colors—now under the great blue wing of nightfall, how exquisite the day's ashes.

No one would notice. Only I knew.

G was fired shortly after. I assumed it had something to do with mistreating the dog.

Just another 'thing' gone missing in that house.

II.

Aunt B

There were a few hours of the day that Mother had allocated purely as her own, for her own. No one was allowed to disturb her then. Not Magan or Kanak or the gardener who might want his monthly dues. Between the hours of two and four in the afternoon, her bedroom door would remain shut. She'd turn on Bengali news for half an hour waiting for the heaviness of the afternoon to descend.

I'd return home at three, to find the crack beneath her door disappear in darkness and would retire to my own room, where I could unravel in privacy—I'd write a letter to a pen pal, or make up a story for my dolls.

At precisely four, sometimes, a quarter past—and then she would tell, whoever would bring her tea, how she had overslept by mistake—the light beneath her door came back on and I could imagine the whole universe in there— the television, the drapes, the tumbler and glasses and unpacked suitcases from my father's many rushed trips—all having awoken up at once.

Some days, she would shower after her tea, put on a

fresh sari, always of a somber print and color, and head down the stairs to her car. Her heels scuffing against the carpet on the staircase importantly. If she had woken up in time, she might peer into my room and tell me she had a meeting or an event to attend.

Time in my house was always divided into two parts—that when my parents were home and all the lights on the ceiling were on and so was the television and all the servants scattered here and there on errands; and that when my parents were not home, away at work, when the lights and fans and sounds switched off and for a brief moment, the house would seem mine.

It was always on those days, at precisely the time my mother's car had rolled out of the garage, and I was ready to feel alive, finally, that Aunt B would arrive.

Aunt B wasn't really my aunt. She was my mother's aunt. A cousin of my grandmother's. But, being younger than my mother, she was too young to be called a grand aunt and possibly for not finding an adequate salutation, I called her 'aunt' as well. Come to think of it, everyone I knew did.

Aunt B was a squat woman and her most prominent feature was her thick lips that were always painted dark Burgundy as though they had been charred by the summer sun. Her hair was always pinned in an eloquent bun at the base of her neck. She never looked up as she carefully hitched her sari and tackled the staircase up to our living room as though she were wading water.

To compliment her features, she had a voice that

sounded as though she were puckering up her tree stump of a nose to make room for decibels. But it wasn't so much the tone as it were the words itself which grate in me.

"Is your Mum-mum at home?" she would ask, almost knowing what the answer would be.

She came every week and each time into a living room taken over by the evening shadows. Yet she never relented. She came at exactly the same time with a blatant hope, desperateness, at the very dark end of daylight, only to turn around disappointed and sadly make her way back—to once again endure her own life.

Some days, she would ask for tea before she heaved her stoutness back to Mayfair Road, the street parallel to us, connected by a narrow lane. It was no more than a five minute walk back to her building—a large white multi-story that looked as grim as a government school. It was across the road from the general store where I would often go to buy chocolates and later cigarettes, and each time I would be weary of the possibility of bumping into her.

I suppose, though, she needed the rest before she dragged her body through the lonely journey back. Perhaps she was wondering which relative's house to go next. Whose printed sofa to sip tea on now. Her plump lips now deflated but still holding on to its last smile.

At first, I would sit on the armrest of the green fabric sofa, which had remained the same color despite surviving many a reupholstering, and politely answer her questions with single words. "Yes, school was fine." "No, I don't know when she will be back."

Aunt B's face was aglow with futile effervescence. You could see her almost willing the answer, "Yes," when she inquired of my mother.

This obscene optimism, perched on her lips—plump with expectation—made me more adamant not to give in to her. So I didn't offer her biscuits and I didn't inquire about her daughter D and I was annoyed that Magan served her tea in the pretty floral pot with plenty of refill, instead of offering her a single cup. After a few minutes, I would excuse myself and go back to my own room. From the corner where I had to turn away from the living room, I could see the back of her bun—held delicately with pins and clips to form whatever semblance of dignity that she could muster up.

Sometimes it would be a good half an hour before I heard her footsteps on the staircase again. Once in a while, if she was really lucky, my mother would return. Then they gossiped about relatives and I could hear her nose grovel at my mother's name, "But you don't know, Chini." She would sing the songs of her grief while my mother patiently listened—to her sorrows, and the sorrows of all their other relations—then, in her curt, precise words, hand out her consolations, her little favors.

Aunt B would say, "I knew you'd know what to do."

Sometimes, my mother made the trip five minutes over to May Fair Road herself. Once a year, when she would clean out her closets, she'd keep piles of saris on different parts of the bed and later, tell Aunt B, "This yellow would look so good on you, I kept it aside just for you."

My mother never spoke of her work with the Ladies Study Group or the Citizens Action Forum with Aunt B. Nor of my father's new ventures. It's as though she brushed aside who she was, to make time for her poorer relative. A form of entertainment—easy and mindless—where she didn't really have to give too much of herself. A real life daytime soap.

Aunt B had a daughter who often came with her.

D was technically my mother's cousin and therefore my aunt but being that she was a few months younger than I, I called her by her name—D. Thankfully the customs of Bengali civility didn't stoop so low as to force me to use a more deferential salutation on her.

The greatest misfortune of Aunt B was actually not her own profuseness, but the existence of D. For I couldn't imagine seeing Aunt B without fearing the possibility of D in our house.

D was a younger, more rounded version of her mother. Where her mother's exuberance would flow out of the folds of her sari, bulging from the edges of her blouse, D's abundance was more contained under her demure salwar, her face not yet having relented to the gravity of years. The worst part about her was that she was actually not a terrible person.

The days D accompanied her mother to our house, I could feel despair settling heavily in my chest. I would have to entertain her as long as my mother decided to entertain Aunt B. Worse were the days when my mother wasn't at home and Aunt B would leave D behind in my care. They didn't have a car, nor spare help at home who could pick her up, so it was left to my mother to arrange for her to return. This meant there was no limit, no foreseeable end to her visit. She stayed as long as my mother allowed her.

What made D most intolerable was her deference. Her compliance in anything I wanted to do. If I wanted to play with the dolls, she would agree. If I wanted to draw, she was awash in eagerness. Her figure replete with submission.

I once sought her help to burn the hair on my Barbie's. We stole a matchbook from my mother's prayer room upstairs and watched the synthetic hair fizzle and char. D didn't say anything. She held a Barbie in her hand and stared at it. Sometimes, she would ask how much they had cost and I would wave away her curiosity by saying, 'I don't know. Baba bought it.'

She would also hold the red pencil case my father had brought back from Japan—with countless hidden compartments for erasers and sharpeners and little clips. She would open the compartments and smell the fragrant erasers. I was used to this kind of scrutiny—in my school no one else wore the kind of socks I did, bought from London, no one had such a pencil case. On one hand was the thrill in owning something special. On the other, was the glaring proof that brought everything spiraling back to a central truth. I was different.

Back in the days before we had Pepsi and cable television and imported chocolates in our corner stores, the only way to get these coveted items was to go to Park Street, where, the shacks at the edge of the road were filled with all sorts of things we only saw in the American movies which we rented from the video stores. On a very special Sunday, my father would drive us there so we could buy a box of stale Kit Kat, which had somehow reached this poor vendor's hands via Dubai and Thailand. They tasted of an arduous journey as well—battered and bruised with expiration dates we ignored by virtue of our mirth. These vendors kept imported cigarettes, after shaves, lighters, electronic goods—all of America, what we later learned was really the Middle East, under one plastic shack.

One year, during Diwali, when our dining table was filled with trousseaus of sweets, cakes and candles, the new Consulate General of Germany, perhaps in trying to make a statement, sent us something quite unique—cases of Coca Cola cans.

We had cola in India. Our domestic version, called Thumbs Up, which had a red and white drawing of a fist with the thumb sticking out. But Coke—that was the thing of films and rock stars' posters—something we knew existed in a far away, parallel world.

Reader, this was akin to having Disneyland be brought to your doorstep, for your and yours only, private use.

My parents, who never touched fast food, measured the soup and salad they ate for dinner, had no interest in such things which meant, I usurped all of it—all thirty six cans.

I rationed them carefully. I never mentioned to visiting friends that there was anything so magnificent in my house. I let them ogle on at my enormous toy collection, the miniature houses, the plastic horses with synthetic hair, never letting on that there was something more physical, more corporeal to the larger world we only theoretically knew existed, in my possession. I would consume one as a reward after completing my schoolwork. Sometimes, on a Sunday as a special treat. I saved the cans afterwards, crushed them to give them what I thought was an 'authentic' look, the kind I aligned with the teen magazines I used to buy from the roadsides on Park Street, and used them as pencil holders. Years later, when my habits became more explorative, they turned into ashtrays, hidden in the nooks of my desk.

One day, at the edge of the afternoon, when time whirled and stirred lazily through the day's absence, while the door crack of my mother's room was still dark, news came via Magan that D had arrived and was downstairs, in the living room. She had obviously been informed by the guards at the gate and the workers that I was at home and there was no point in trying to hide in the ocean of jasmine pots my mother grew in the terrace, craning my neck to watch her retreat back out through the gate. Reluctantly, I headed down, dragging myself over each step in submission.

D was sitting erect on the sofa, one hand resting on the other across her lap, her hair swept back dutifully with a plastic hairband, glistening of oil that her mother must have applied on her, looking nowhere in particular.

"Hi," she said, as she saw me emerge through the shadows of respite. I wondered how to entertain her that day. Should I bring out the dolls? The coloring books? Should we play around the house so I could hide in obscure corners till it was time for her to leave?

There was nothing as sorrowful and sweet as the fullness of solitude and D had interrupted mine.

Magan lingered around annoyingly.

"Does Didi want a drink?" he asked.

I looked at her.

"Sure," she said.

"Is there any Thumbs Up in the house?" I asked him.

"Dekchhi," he said. I'll look.

I wondered how and when D would leave that day. I had no control of her departure, to decide when it was enough, my freedom contingent on someone else's mercy.

Magan still lingered annoyingly. Then he said something—so simple and innocent you'd think he truly had my best interest in mind. "Didi," he said, "Oi Coca Cola ta acche." Didi, we have that Coca Cola.

I had a great talent—in moments of extreme calamity or shock—I never screamed or cried out loud. Instead, I went inside myself. I hid all my emotions behind the stone of my spine and could make my face look as plain as a wall, even though all the while my heart might have been trying to push itself out.

To my greatest relief, D shook her pristine, oiled head and with remarkable poise said, "That's okay a Thumbs Up will do."

Magan said he would go have a look.

The metal object which had risen up to my throat, now dissolved into a light ball of air into my stomach.

We turned around and walked towards my bedroom, where I would now have to entertain her till the world came to an end.

She walked behind me, in her white kameez with yellow printed flowers, the cotton of the fabric clinging to the folds of her sides, her mounded stomach, her courteous footsteps following me towards whatever it was that I would decide would be our mission for the evening.

Suddenly, she stopped and she turned around.

"Actually, if it's such a huge problem, I wouldn't mind a Coca Cola either." I stopped too.

She looked at me as though it was nothing at all, as though it were she who was doing me a favor—relieving me of a burden. Through the gauze of civility, she had bestowed on me a kind of authority I didn't want. Because, of course, now it was up to me to do the correct thing. Truth was, it were I who was powerless in this situation, having been cornered against the wall of liability and obligation. How could I say 'No'?

Something hot rose up my spine but I didn't let it show. This wasn't about D or even the imported cans. She could have simply said she really wanted a Coke. I would have acquiesced even though I might not have wanted to. She could have widened her eyes, restless with questions, and vomit her feelings out—that she too wanted a taste of America, that she'd like to take back a crushed can of her own. But she didn't. Instead, she, using frailty as her weapon, left me with the duty to change the world.

I looked as plainly at her as she had at me. Her eyes were shining and full of begging and that made me feel more defenseless.

Between her and me and the shrapnel of her good manners, I could say anything. I was in that position.

I had never wanted that power, that kind of responsibility.

"Of course not, it's no problem at all. There's plenty of Thumbs Up in the house," I said.

I turned around and headed to my bedroom full of things, all kinds of miracles in my visitor's eyes.

'I wouldn't mind.'

The words so meager. She uttered them as though she knew what they meant. Nothing is more natural than wanting things. Nothing sillier and more desolate.

Back in my room, I took out my large collection of dolls—mangled and twisted into a large shopping bag— white and blue. D drank her Thumbs Up with timid sips. She didn't complain when I gave her the doll with a malfunctioning arm. The problem with D was that she never complained at all. You almost wanted to shake her, tell her to say it, let it out like a man's red spittle on the roadside—all the pride that we grit between our breath.

All evening and the night beyond seemed to have gone by before my mother's voice was heard, forceful yet soft, like July rain, announcing that Magan was ready to escort D back. My companion got up—all of her shiny, excessive self. She brushed out her kameez. A scent of soap and powder falling from its folds. On her chin, a light brown water mark. The spoils of her aspirations.

I didn't point it out.

"Bye," she called out from the staircase. Her cheeks abundant with gratitude.

I returned to my room, breathing as though someone had just unplugged my ribcage.

'I don't mind.'

Whatever is invisible is never really absent.

Outside, you could hear the evening birds start their call. The Aajan from the mosque nearby. Window shutters closed their heavy eyelids.

Everything went about its way, its rules, its everyday ordinariness.

III.

THE VISIT

In September, Anita left Mark. She wrote out instructions for Maya, packed two bags and took a taxi to Hopkins Airport in Cleveland. From there, she flew down to New York's LaGuardia.

Ohio spread below like a chequer board of green and brown. East coast rolled so close she could smell it like rain. It was only for two weeks. Two weeks that permitted, no matter how fleeting, the smallest thrill of betrayal.

The key, as Anjali had promised, was with the doorman who, in his grey suit and fixed stare, made Anita feel shabby after the long journey from Columbus. She gave him her name, signed the visitor's register and as she hustled her duffle bag and carry-on into the elevator, was distinctly aware of him watching her struggle.

The last time she had stayed with Anjali was somewhere else—downtown perhaps. Anjali was always moving, changing neighbourhoods—the way one changed their wardrobe when they got bored or it felt out of fashion. Mark and Anita had lived in the same house on Beaumont Road for as long as they had been together. Eight years. Eight years and they had never bothered to paint the kitchen, as she had always wanted—Lemondrop Yellow. She didn't mind the creased walls anymore. She had long come to an understanding with it. There was something about living around acres of land and wide blue skies that felt fixed and settled.

She unlocked the door to the apartment and set the keys down on the entry table. It tumbled out of her hand and skated across the smooth surface. Quickly she picked them up, worried she may have accidentally scratched the polished mahogany. At least, that is what she thought such wood was called. Whenever nice furniture was described in magazines, they always said mahogany. She knew because she used to stare at the pictures, then discreetly, without Mark noticing, search the pages for their prices, which were always written in the smallest of fonts at the very bottom.

When they had first moved into that house on Beaumont, Mark constantly told her it was better to buy from local flea markets—one found decent, solid pieces, reasonably priced, which they only had to sand down or wax or distress if they so wished. He had hair back then, long and straight, that always strayed on the sides. But everything else about him was contained: his taste for spices—he had a sensitive stomach; the way he ate—he cut everything into the smallest of pieces; his words—he rationed them just like his food and sometimes Anita blabbed on just to get a satisfactory response out of him; even the white T-shirt he always wore hung from his lean frame with austere athleticism.

The foyer of Anjali's apartment opened out on both ends and Anita followed it to the left, which led her into the living room. The south-facing wall was entirely windowed, with blue fabric shades, Roman shades they were called, that ballooned at the bottom. She had wanted shades like those, not in blue but in a pale yellow and not rounded at the bottom but straight. She had seen them in the 'Country Curtains' catalogue.

Mark had said "No." He had said, "Imagine how stupid they'd look in our living room with the metal futon and the scratched-up table."

"Why will they look stupid?"

"Because you can't do up half the room and not the rest."

"What's wrong with that? It's kind of nice to have one good thing. It's like wearing pretty underwear beneath track-pants."

Mark didn't think that was funny. He didn't think there was any point in wearing pretty underwear either. He said they came off in the end, anyway. So Anita brought back curtains from India. The pillowcases too were from there. It was true, they never had much of a budget to work with but she was proud that she managed, in her efficient way, to always make do.

This house was not like hers—a collage of salvaged fabrics. Every surface of this room, and there were several of them, were filled with photo frames and ornaments and books and bowls. Anjali's house in Calcutta was much like this as well, only larger. She used to be scared of that house, of the large dining room on the ground floor—with its wood panels and crystal chandeliers and oil paintings in gold frames. It felt old and when something was that old, she thought ghosts hid behind the walls.

They used to play a game called 'Dark Room' in there—hide-and-seek with all the lights turned off. Anjali always made her the first seeker.

When it was her turn, she stood outside the mirrored doors of the dining room. Then she'd open the doors and plunge herself into the deep dark room.

This trip was like plunging.

She parked her bags in a corner of the room where they looked more worn down against the plump, upholstered sofa. She hadn't been thinking when she had grabbed them from the upper shelf of their narrow hall closet—stowed away alongside Mark's old laptop carrier, his piles of vintage records, the old shoe-boxes stuffed with power cords, broken gadgets, batteries, whatever had fit. The bags were coated with stains—years of filth collected while moving one apartment to another, from being hauled up endless flights of stairs, and now, from the baby, who staked her claim on every conceivable surface. At the thought of Maya, Anita felt the prick of guilt. Not for having left but for failing to mourn in the ways mothers were meant to mourn the absence of their children.

On the other side of the long hallway, past the entry, was a door that led into a bathroom. Her eyes fixed on the Jacuzzi tub. Somewhere, at the back of her head, she could hear Mark's voice, "Annie, baths are such a waste of water. There's nothing wrong with a shower-stall. They've got perfectly good water pressure and are a breeze to clean." He would say this not sternly, as an admonishment. Rather, explain it the way she might explain the sun and the moon to Maya.

A subtle fragrance in the air, like a mild afternoon wind that carried with it the smell of summer flowers. Perhaps, she would go for a massage in the city, before Mark and Maya came down. It had been so long since she had pampered herself.

Past the bathroom was another door. On it, a sticky-note addressed to her:

Hi honey,

This is your room. Make yourself at home. Your bathroom is down the hallway and I've kept out your towels. Kitchen's a bit empty unfortunately but feel free to help yourself to whatever you want. I'll be back from my trip late evening (flight lands at eight) and then we have some much needed catching up to do.

Love,

A.

Catching up. How exactly would they do that? She could summarize her life in a few sentences: What have you been up to? Oh nothing. I wake up and feed Maya. We play. She takes naps. She wakes and I feed her again. In between I read catalogues and magazines that Mark doesn't approve of. In the evening, he comes home and goes straight to his desk. Then I take the dildo to the bathroom.

So much had happened over the years. Anjali and she had kept in touch at first—through intermittent emails, a phone-call every few months, a visit when possible.

Mostly it was Anita who came down to New York, where Anjali studied, from her college town of Delaware. Delaware, Ohio—you could squeeze that name like stale lemon and nothing would come out. The woman at the ticket-counter in Port Authority had once said, "I'm sorry, we don't go there." But Anita told her she was wrong. She told the woman that the bus did indeed go there—from New York to Cleveland, from where one would have to change to a bus to Columbus and finally to a third, that went into Delaware.

In the days to come she would remind Anjali of those stories. They would reminisce about the old days. She would tell her that Menaka had gotten a divorce—the first of their lot. That was to be expected though. After all, she had started much earlier than the rest of them.

Anita rummaged through her handbag, which was filled to the brim with her toothbrush, toothpaste, face wash, all the things that hadn't fit in her luggage. She dug out her phone and dialed Mark's number. "Hey," she said when he answered in his familiar, unhurried speech.

"Heyy. Missing me already, huh?"

"No. It's not that," she said, somewhat stiffly. Mark had told her right from the start that she wouldn't be able to stay away from them. He had told her that they should just bite the bullet and move to the city together and use their saving while they both hunted for new jobs. It would only be for a month, two at the most. But he hadn't thought things through. In spite of all his good sense, he never considered the real practical matters such as medical costs, which were far higher in New York. They weren't on friendly terms with any doctors here, as they were with their local pediatrician in Columbus. Besides, child-care was outrageously expensive in the city while they had such a strong support-system back home—what with Greta and Joy and Carrie and Dennis— all their neighbours who were only too eager to help; the sort of community living she had, at one time, longed for— in the same way she had always dreamed of sitting by an evening fire, with a shawl over her lap. No one had told her then that her fires would be all smoke and ash.

Anita had insisted that Mark stay back with Maya, in Columbus. She said he should continue working at the bookshop while she move ahead for her upcoming job interview and try to sort out their living situation. Once the bookshop closed down and his position officially terminated, he and Maya could join her. Hopefully by then she would have found something.

Found some answers at least.

They had discussed things through and he knew how

important it was for her to find the right situation this time—a career, not just a job—perhaps working at a small non-profit or, if she was lucky, at a gallery or museum. She had told Mark she couldn't do it anymore—live in quiet submission, away from people, the noise of a city. She had told him that her emotional wellbeing was important for their future, even if it meant making small sacrifices now. They had been deliberating this shift to New York for some time now. Then came the announcement that the bookshop would close in the fall and they knew it was time to make that big change.

Nothing ever changes.

Mark's voice hummed over the phone, like an old, scratchy song turning on a record player.

"Did Maya have all her food this morning?" she asked.

"Mostly. She didn't like the carrots. She spit them on the floor."

"She always does that with carrots."

"She doesn't like them."

"No. She doesn't like them at all."

"But you could try mixing them with apple-sauce," she added. "She loves that. If you run out, get the ones with the green packaging. Not the other kind they carry at the store. She doesn't like those as much."

"Apple-sauce in pink packaging," Mark repeated, slowly. He may have been writing it down. He had a bad memory and she always made him write out lists. She had, once, even made him a list of all the things she'd wanted him to do in bed. But he had looked at her with disgust and said that's not what he was—a toy that turned on and off at her bidding.

"Green, green. Not pink."

"Green," he repeated. "Okay. Got it."

"And make sure you rub on the cream after her bath. Or else she gets that rash."

"I know. I remember."

What else? What else could she talk of now? She was tired of talking about baby food. Sometimes, she felt the world was passing by and all she ever did was change diapers. She wanted to talk about real things like that last conversation they had, three years ago, when Anita was last down in the city. On that trip, she had confessed to her friend that Mark and she were not having as much sex as she would like. She hadn't meant to talk about that but after the second glass of wine, it somehow felt right.

"We do have sex of course," Anita had added, "It's just not the same as before. He's always writing at night and even when we do get it on, it's a bit perfunctory."

To her relief, Anjali didn't round her eyes and lower her voice to a ribbon like whisper and say, "Really?" She shook her head tragically and told her she knew all about complacent marriages. She had heard this story so many times. "Yes, sex is important," she said. "You just need a good fuck now and again, you know?"

They were at a restaurant on the fiftieth floor of a building. The room was dark. After her second glass of wine, the stars and lights outside the panoramic windows melded with the walls and she felt as though she were floating. "Yes." Anita had said. "Yes, that's what I need. A good fuck. I should tell Mark that. I should just say, Mark, fuck me."

"And then, you know, there are accessories," Anjali had said.

"What kind of accessories?"

"Oh many. Like leather underwear with a hole in it."

"That's disgusting."

"It's not disgusting. It's kinky. Men like kinky," Anjali said. She also said that older men didn't like women to shave down there.

"Not even the bikini line? I would never ever do a full Brazilian but at least the bikini line."

"Trust me. They prefer it natural!" She leaned forward and lowered her voice as she said this.

That was the last time the two had met. Then Maya was born and her life spiralled somewhere else. Anjali couldn't make it for the rice ceremony—she was on a business trip to Hong Kong—but she sent a gold locket with an engraved heart pendant. On Maya's first birthday—for which they had rented La Cucina, the best Italian restaurant in town and Anita had taken cake-baking lessons for three months— she couriered a tricycle.

"Annie, you there? You're really quiet."

"Sorry. I was just thinking. I should go now. I just got here," she said. "Call me later, after you put Maya to bed, okay?"

"Okay."

"Okay?"

"Okay, okay. I said okay."

"I was just making sure."

"Bye Annie. And please don't drive yourself crazy. We're doing fine here. Just fine."

"I know, I know," she sighed loudly. This silent voicing of discontent was the only way she could try and talk to him now.

She pictured Mark giving their daughter a bath that night, reading to her, turning the lights off and the blinds down. Not that he didn't help with those things when she was there. He did. They shared in all the household duties equally. He was truly amazing. Her rock. No. Her coconut tree—bald and simple.

She was lucky to have found Mark. She really was. She had friends whose husbands never lifted a finger.

But this was also what she wanted. Mark said she was conflicted but all she really needed was a little time. Soon, everything would be normal again.

"Talk later," Mark said, the words stretched, lethargic, a pace that was in good contrast to her worrying nature, a pace that unfortunately permeated into the bedroom as well.

It also promised, in its own way, that everything would turn out fine. Everything did in fact always turn out fine. But only because Anita worked hard at them. She had worked hard at finding a job in the HR department of a small law firm in Columbus—not one she enjoyed but at least one with decent benefits; she made monthly budgets when Mark went part-time so he could focus on his writing; rationed their outings; resisted urges to buy new clothes; learned to drive so she could get herself to her old university in Delaware where she used her alumni discount to take fitness classes. When New York became a real possibility, she job hunted till darkness dragged over the streets and silence blared through the house. She proofed her cover letters over and over and even pleasured herself in the bathroom on those nights she knew Mark was not in the mood. Every night. She worked and worked and gave and gave. She was proud of it. Life could never defeat her. She was a fighter, a survivor and everything became more bearable when Maya cast her first look at the world into her mother's eyes. Although it had been just three years, Anita couldn't remember a life before motherhood. Maya was her equilibrium. She had no regrets. She really didn't. In fact, if anything, she should have had her earlier.

* * *

Anjali's building was on the Upper West Side. You walked out and turned left and came up to the chaos of Broadway. There was an organic market at the corner—yellow, green, orange fruits and buckets of lilies, roses, tulips, daisies and carnations lay heaving outside in voluptuous bins. In front, the din of traffic criss crossed the two-way avenue; further ahead—the heavy artillery of construction. One block over, Amsterdam Avenue was lined in restaurants with foreign names and outdoor seating and umbrellas over which the evening sun scattered.

A little boutique on the corner of 82nd Street caught Anita's attention—the window dressed in pink wallpaper, lined with mannequins in multi-coloured hair wearing black clothes and platform boots. It stood out from the other shops that sold khaki coats and tapered pants and lace-trimmed children's wear. She stopped in front of it. Not the sort of clothes she typically wore. But window-shopping wasn't about looking at what you had in mind. It was looking for what you could never imagine.

There was one dress though, that she thought she could potentially wear. The skirt was ordinary and long, ending just below the knee of the mannequin. It would come farther down on her smaller frame. It opened out into a wide 'A' line that would hide her gradually expanding hips at all stages of life. What gave the dress an edge, the right to be displayed up there, along with the leather pants and corsets, was its top—a tight halter-necked bodice showing off a large portion of the back and a thin vinyl strap with a gold buckle.

She was tempted to go into the store but stopped herself. Reminded herself that all these clothes were made somewhere in Bangladesh or South America—produced in bulk, shipped in hordes. They didn't hold the intrigue of time and memory that cleaved the racks of vintage stores. Besides, that dipping neckline was too low.

She walked on. She walked three more blocks and came up to the burgundy awning of a restaurant. Through its tinted windows, votives flapped above white linen and behind them, the dancing shadows of sinewy bodies. It was Friday evening. The weekend had begun.

Anita looked down in dismay at her own attire—light blue jeans of a nondescript origin; a plain, purple T-shirt; a brown bag picked up after much haggling with a street vendor. She might as well have worn an 'I LOVE NY' cap to go with it. Somewhere along Amsterdam, there must be a pizza place, a Chinese take-out. They were usually in every corner, like the foliage of New York City. She walked in what must have been circles—through the side streets that tunnelled endlessly, shadowed by the spread of Honeylocusts and Willows that gave the fleeting impression of something green and serene, then out again into the grey, concrete discord of the avenue. Windows lit up. Restaurants glowed under candles. The sky turned pink but a different sort of light took over the city. Soon, she was back in front of the shop with pink wallpaper. She had walked for almost an hour. Her feet were heavy and hot. Now, in the dusk, the neckline of the dress didn't look so bad after all.

She lightly pushed the door open. The bell rang. The

woman behind the register looked up, tentatively, as though she didn't want to unsettle the bright blue wig and the silver tiara that balanced on her head.

"Hey there," she said. Her voice, like her hair was coloured—first husky, then ending on a high note—a voice that had been resting for quite some time. Anita thought she must have walked into a Halloween shop. But it was too late. The woman had looked up. She felt she had to stay for a while and look.

The shop was larger than it had appeared from the outside. It was narrow but ran deep and was divided into two sections—the front for a large assortment of dark clothes and the back for sparkled shoes and bright wigs and fake eyelashes— accessories necessitated by morbid clothing, she imagined.

She browsed the racks and ran her fingers lightly over every item, making it known that she was considering each of the black dresses and lace tops and vinyl corsets, which she had no idea how to put on because there was too much of criss crossing of lace at the back. The blue-haired woman was sitting at the register. Every time Anita looked at her, she quickly put her head down and proceeded to untangle the heap of price tags in her hand.

Between the meshed nylons, she finally found the black dress she had seen earlier in the window. It looked much narrower than it did on the mannequin but Anita couldn't help herself from searching for the price.

"We're having a sale," the woman said. "That whole rack

is fifty per cent off." Her voice had finally found its happy medium.

Anita nodded. Another minute and it would be okay to leave.

"Why don't you try it?"

"Oh no, that's okay. I was just looking."

"Really. Just try it."

"No, that's fine. Thank you."

The blue-haired woman came out from behind the register. She wore leopard-printed leggings under a short black skirt. Her legs were thick, like tree trunks.

"Darling. There's nothing wrong with just trying. Really. What size are you? A medium?"

Anita wanted to say 'small', which was her original size, but the truth was, she hadn't fit into anything small since Maya was born.

"Let me see. Look. That's a medium," the woman said. She held out the dress over her own body and twirled gaily, as if all day long she'd wanted to do just that.

"No really, that's okay."

"Tsk," the woman shook her head. "You see what's written on my shirt? Read it. Come on now. Read it. Don't be shy."

"It's all about me," Anita read out loud.

"Now read the back."

"I forgot about you."

"You see that?" the woman flipped her hand. "It's all about you girl. When's the last time you said that? Now I know you like that dress. I can see it in your eyes."

The dress was even tighter than what Anita had expected, especially around the hip. But that, in fact, made the fabric cling around her butt, which she knew was her asset (Mark used to say so back in the day). From the front, it was demure and simple. Only when she turned around was the open back fully exposed and could one see the vinyl strap with the little gold buckle, which nestled behind her neck like a secret. She imagined what Mark would say. He wouldn't make her return it of course, or say anything openly negative. He wasn't that sort of a man. But she knew he'd silently judge her, in the same way he said Hollywood movies or her friend, Anjali.

"So? What do you think?" the blue-haired woman asked from behind the curtain of the changing room. "It's fifty per cent off, so it's only eighty-five."

Over the next two weeks, Anjali and she would do all the things they'd done together in the past—go to restaurants serving fusion cuisine, to bars with blue lights and cocktails in martini glasses, perhaps even to a party that Anjali was invited to.

"There's tax of course, but it's still an incredible bargain."

She could wear this dress out one night. She could keep the tag on and return it afterwards. They could both dress up as they used to. Right up to their hair. Yes. Wouldn't that be something? Sometimes, Anita felt there was an actress in a sequined brassier and hips that swayed like a snake hiding inside her, dying to be let out when Mark wasn't looking.

The blue-haired woman folded the dress in pink tissue. First one side laid carefully and flat, then the other—pulled snug, the way Anita pulled at Maya's coat over a thick sweater in the winter. Finally, a little pink sticker on the top. She threw in a box of blue eye shadow and winked. "That's for you honey, for helping me to reach the day's target. Now I can close the store early."

The sun had slipped behind the tall buildings. Darkness fell, as it does— gradually, then all at once. People were heading out for dinner—in pairs, in groups, arm-in-arm, footstep-to-footstep, conversations churned the air. A girl stopped outside the shop. She was talking loudly into her phone.

"What do you think?" she said. "He went for more booze of course…three vodkas so far. And a pretzel…God! It's way steamy out here. I'm a bit drunk." She giggled. "Just one but you know how I get with just a glass of wine…yes, he is…yes, I hope so too…his place, we're right here…I hope he makes a pretzel out of me."

Anita stopped the blue-haired woman, as she was about to put the dress in a shopping bag. "You know what? I'd like to wear that dress right now, if that's okay."

* * *

The restaurant was French, a name she wanted to pronounce as 'cute' but she knew it wasn't that. It was probably 'cue'. Or worse. She was probably way off. It wasn't the kind of name she was used to seeing—Le Chateau for example. Everybody knew how to say that.

It was still relatively early for dinner in New York, but many of the tables were filled. Waiters sieved through the dark wood furniture with trays tucked under their arms. The lights were turned low and the cutlery shone under the candles. The hostess, who was standing near the bar, looked up from her reservations book and smiled—not the generous kind, which she probably saved for the prime-time clientele and regulars, but with a certain reservation, possibly directed at the stragglers who walked in with none.

"Are you waiting for someone?" she asked.

"No. No, it's just me."

She was led to the far side of the room, the part that was mostly unoccupied—where tables of twos were set against the wall—like the empty side of a stadium. Menus were brought over and set down. Not thrown, but with careful disinterest. While she read through it, Anita couldn't help but notice the two waiters hovering to her side. Her back felt cold. She shook out her hair to cover it. She had thought once she sat down she would feel better, but if anything, the clanking of glasses, of forks against plates, the grating of chairs and raised conversations from the other, busier side, heightened their absence from her end. Getting up and leaving would look more absurd.

Instead of 'appetizers', the menu had something called 'Amuse-Gueules'. She supposed they were appetizers because they were the only things within her price range—grilled calamari with fennel, country paté, some kind of a dish with baked Brie, a large selection of salads. Everything else was quite exorbitant.

It had been some time since Anita had indulged herself to a good dinner. With real food. When they had first met, Mark used to frown on her unhealthy Indian eating habits, which consisted chiefly of fried potatoes and over-spiced curries. He encouraged her (in his wonderfully gentle and inspiring way) to try healthier things such as steamed squash and tofu. She had grown to enjoy that sort of food—which she discovered was excellent for digestion—just as she had traded in the glossy magazines for The New Yorker. Mark said it was the only magazine worth spending money on. They took turns reading their subscription copy and afterwards, at night, when Maya was asleep, discussed some of the articles.

"Have you read this story, Annie? He's one of my favourite writers," Mark had said.

"Yes, I did. I loved it."

"Oh yeah? Really?" Mark sat up. Anything about literature excited him. Sometimes, it seemed to Anita, he was more aroused by Baldwin and Borges than by breasts. "What did you think? What did you like about it?"

"Oh, I don't know," she said. Her voice became hesitant with the burden of having to prove herself. "It was…you know…touching."

"You found it touching?"

"Well no. Not touching exactly. But it moved me."

After some thinking, Anita said, "I like the way he looks at things."

"Sensibility."

"What?"

"An artist's sensibility," Mark said, using the sort of voice he did with some of the people that came into his bookshop—not patronizing really, or preacher-ish, but as if he were rehearsing for his future teaching career."

After some deliberation, Anita finally decided on the escargot—a good, economical choice, she thought. Not the cheapest, which might show a lacking, but reasonable enough and far more exciting than salad, which was likely to be what Mark would have ordered.

It was what lovers popped into each other's mouth. Why did she just think that? She wasn't sure. Something about the rolling of the 'r' in 'escargot' felt sensuous and illicit.

The waiter had forgotten to take the wine-list back. Or perhaps he had intentionally left it behind. Anita flipped through it. She thought, while she was on the path of self-indulgence, she might as well go all the way. She summoned the waiter.

"Could I get a glass of red wine, please?" she whispered.

"Sorry? What?" He leaned closer.

She looked to her left, then to her right. "Red wine. You know…" she whispered again, a little louder this time.

"Any particular kind?" he asked and she wished he would lower his voice.

She looked through the list again. None of the names meant anything to her. "Merlot," she said, because it was what she usually drank. When she did. Mark and she weren't the drinking kind. Well, Mark wasn't. She loved wine. But it wasn't much fun to drink alone.

Several other people had come in by then and her section of the room was starting to get busy. She hadn't realized before how closely all the tables were set together—side-by-side, with barely a few inches between them. She was the only one who sat alone, separated from the din of the room, against the wall, in exile.

Her wine arrived and she took a sip right away. It felt good.

This was right. This was everything she'd fought against to get here. "Excuse me," a voice said from behind.

"Oh sorry." She pulled her chair closer to make room. A man passed through and sat at the table to her left. They were seated so close that if she moved a little to that side, her dress would touch the leg of his chair, or their arms might accidentally rub. But she couldn't see his face. In order to do so, she'd have to turn deliberately in his direction.

All she could see were his white sleeves, which rested on the menu but didn't open it; all she could hear was a voice that spoke in the lowest octave, saying something to the waiter who took the menu and went away. Then he got up and reached in his leather bag, which was on the other chair, across from him, and she thought—what a fine ass he has.

Eventually, unable to bear it any longer, she circled her neck as if stretching it and gave the room a brief survey. She hadn't noticed the wrought iron candelabras hanging from the ceiling before. Or the white flowers on every table. Le Chateau had roses. She never did like roses. They smelt too sweet. As she turned her head, she let her eyes slide over the next table as though it was just one more thing.

Their eyes met and the man smiled at her, an acknowledgement that they were two fellow diners, eating by themselves on a Friday night. The lines on the sides of his face—dark; his hair combed back from his wide, receding forehead. He looked good in his white shirt. Another button undone would have been better. Then he'd look quite dashing, in a Anjali's old lover sort of way.

God. When did she start finding creases sexy?

He flipped pages as if he were looking for a bullet point—a bunch of papers held together in a black clasp. A business brief? Manuscript? She wished she had a magazine. There was something so desperate about a woman eating dinner by herself on a weekend night. Or she should have waited for Anjali's flight to land. If Anjali were here, she'd have started a conversation with the man already. Actually, she wouldn't even need to. He'd be the one to say something first. And then she'd start on her questions, like running water. She'd ask him what he did. When he told her he was a corporate lawyer at Wells Fargo, she'd ask him how their new east coast expansion had worked out. She knew something about everything. They'd talk the whole night through and every once in a while she'd look at Anita and say, "Don't you think so?" There'd come a time when it might seem quite outrageous that Anita had considered him at all.

In between turning pages, the man reached for his wine without looking up. His hands didn't so much as even grope, it just knew where to go, as it knows parts of its own body. Her wine was done. She might as well get another. She raised her hand to call for the waiter.

Few minutes later, the busboy carried out her escargot. Instead of bringing it to her, he served it to the man who looked up, puzzled.

"I think that's mine," Anita said.

"Oh. Sorry," the busboy stuttered and took it around.

"New guy," the man said, shaking his head when the busboy left. "They always get these stupid new guys."

She laughed and looked away. Why did she do that? She always did that.

The man was back to reading. He flipped a black pen in his hand like a baton. His heel tapped against the floor.

"Well, you know, we single diners…we probably all look the same," she laughed.

Alone. That's what she had meant.

"Right," he said.

"You probably thought it was on the house or something."

He nodded and smiled and looked down at his work. His cheeks were shadowed. She felt better now—the confidence that comes after a glass of wine, in new surroundings and a backless dress. The escargot was warm and slippery in her mouth.

"This is good."

The man still had his head down but she knew he was aware of her, in the same way she knew the bartender and the old woman at the table in front had noticed that she was sitting alone.

"It's really delicious."

"Sorry?" he looked up. "Were you saying something?"

"The escargot. It's very good."

"Yes…yes."

"It's very detectable."

The man's eyebrows dipped together like the arms of a bow.

"I mean delectable."

"Yes…"

"The flavours are very…interesting."

"Uh, yes. They like to be a little innovative out here."

"Yes. Very innovative," she said. Her voice had started to do that jumpy sort of thing. She needed to stop getting so excited. Mark always said she got excited easily. Oh Mark.

She dipped bread into the sauce at the bottom of the plate. It dripped on the table and she dabbed it with her napkin. She folded the napkin over so the stain was hidden and put it back on her lap. She pulled it to the left to make it even. Then a little to the right. The man was still flipping pages.

"Your food is taking quite long," she said.

He looked up again and let out a strong exhalation— like a bull. No, a wild horse. A fuming stallion. "Well, I think that's just the steak being cooked—they usually take a while," he said.

"Yeah."

He pursed his lips, as though he wanted to smile more fully but circumstances prevented him—a wife; a loveless marriage that had outlived its course. She imagined he spent many hours at this restaurant, wading in his sea of papers, in order to avoid returning to the perdition of the four walls that caved in on his life. He couldn't leave because of the children—duties, promises— she knew how that worked. Somewhere in his eyes, she saw a quiet grieving.

She took another sip of wine. She'd almost finished the second glass. Something was rising up through her abdomen. If she closed her eyes, she could feel it moving up her chest, lifting her as though she was tied to the wings of a thousand birds. She swept her hair to one side and leaned forward. Her hand brushed against the gold buckle behind her neck. She felt at any given moment anything could happen to change her life forever.

She leaned over and whispered, "I think it's because we're sitting alone, you know? I think there's some conspiracy against single diners."

Alone, alone, dammit.

"Um, yeah, sure," he said. He lowered his head again and turned pages briskly.

The room was buzzing. She could feel her eyes glaze and tried to focus on something steady, the wall. There was a ceramic plate hanging on it. A blue ship set out on the sea—with its sails swollen in the wind, its oars swiping through the water. It wasn't a pirate ship. Majestic towers rose over its masts and flags blew merrily in the wind. A happy ship; on its way to an adventure.

If she stayed like this, as though with blinkers on either side of her face, then it wasn't so bad. Everything around her went away and the buzz faded and she felt as if she were the only one in the restaurant. And the miserable man. She felt a certain responsibility towards him, to show him that the future was long and uncertain and it was that prospect of uncertainty for which they must strive on. She leaned closer. "You want to try some?"

"Sorry?"

"Escargot. Try some."

"Ah…no. That's fine. Thank you."

"Really, try some. Just dip some bread in the sauce."

"I have my steak coming, but thank you for your offer."

"Seriously. I don't mind."

"That's okay."

"Well, if you change your mind, I'm right here. I mean, it's right here."

"Um, yeah," he said.

"Yeah." She took another swig of the merlot. She should have drunk more slowly because now she had to go to the restroom. The weight of the wine had settled down in her pelvis. She got up and smoothened out the dress and made sure she walked around her table and passed from his front. Without looking up, he pulled the table closer towards him to make room. She knew he'd do that.

"I'm just going to the restroom," she said. She didn't need to say it but she had wanted to. Had wanted to let him know that she wasn't abandoning him. As she walked away, she could feel his eyes light up her body.

If Anjali were here, they'd have both gotten up together. While Anita went into the toilet, Anjali would lean forward and suck in her cheeks and examine her face in the mirror. Then she'd stand back and examine her full body. They wouldn't giggle or gossip as other girls did. They'd leave all that for later, when they went home. Just as they would tonight. Only an hour now. Well, perhaps two, there might be traffic.

She opened her bag to take out her lipstick and saw the

green light on her phone winking surreptitiously from its cubby. Mark! She had forgotten all about him. Over from a blanched Columbus night, her husband was calling to let her know that he'd put their child to sleep and turned the phone on silent and drawn the curtains and switched off all the main lights and was about to retreat on his easy chair for the next two hours with Anna Karenina (he was rereading Tolstoy lately).

It wasn't Mark. It was Anjali. "Darling. It's me," she said on the message. 'I'm really sorry but I won't be able to make it tonight. I have to stay back here a little longer. I might be back next week sometime, I'm not sure. Something's come up. I'm really sorry. But don't let that change your plans. Stay as long as you need to. Make yourself at home. If you need anything ask the doorman. My cleaning lady will come day after. She'll look after the house so you don't have to worry about a thing. And to make it up, I've booked you a day at the Bliss Spa in Midtown. I insist. Really. Once you settle in, call them to make an appointment. They have my card. Bye. I miss you."

She shouldn't be disappointed. This wasn't Anjali's fault after all. But now what was she to do with the dress? Or the evenings she'd set aside? The long trip from Columbus felt so pointless. She wondered where Anjali was. She never had mentioned. Sooner or later, Anita would find out anyway. She'd find pictures on a blog, an online article in Conde Nast Traveller about spontaneous traveling, perhaps some comments or a link on a mutual friend's Facebook profile. She'd sit on her bed, in the obscurity of nightfall— when

Maya had long given in to the gentle rhythms of her dreams, and Mark was a quotation mark over his desk— pouring over every little detail, till she imagined that Anjali herself had told her all of it. This was how they had remained close throughout the years, even though they'd never met. This is how they'd always stay in each other's lives—acquainted just enough so that they never slipped into an obscure acquaintanceship. The Internet was an incredible thing.

Before going out, Anita retouched her lipstick, smoothened out her hair and practiced her smile—she mustn't show her teeth when she went back out. She had to remember that. Refined women always smiled demurely, with little show of anything. She rehearsed her smile again. One more time. There, that was the one. She reasoned that if she bought herself some time, the man's steak might arrive and they might finish dinner at exactly the same time. Nothing came for free in life. One had to create their opportunities. She knew that. She was a fighter. So now, if she coordinated this exit well, then on their way out of the restaurant, the man would hold the door open for her. She would wait for a taxi, even though Anjali's apartment was near-by. He'd ask her where she was going.

"Oh a little ways off," she would say. A well-told lie was necessary, not a crime.

He'd say he had just finished working on a big case and was going down to Gramercy.

"I'm staying with a friend," she'd say.

"You're not from here then?" he'd ask.

"Actually, I'm staying at her place while she isn't here."

Then he'd ask, since she was not doing anything else, if she would like to have a drink together.

"Oh, I don't know. It's kind of late."

There wouldn't be too many taxis at that time but one would happen to pull up to let someone out. He'd get in and hold the door open for her and she'd say, "Oh well, okay, just one." She'd suck in her cheeks and throw her hips forward.

They would cut across the park—the streetlights snaking through the long winding road. Tall trees on either side making the night feel heavy. They would ride in silent acquiescence towards something inevitable.

Down the wide Park Avenue, the traffic lights would blink their lonely warnings, a bicyclist would ride by, pedalling furiously and paying no attention, windows would drop down their shades, preparing for a new chapter in the morning. Ultimately, they would come to a stop on a side street. It would be a brownstone building with a green awning and heavy glass doors with white frames. Must be a pied-a-terre he owned in the city she'd imagine. There'd be a long hallway with chequered floors and a mirror to the right. But no doorman. Doormen always led to unnecessary conversation and then awkwardness. As they walked to the elevator, at the far end of the hall, she would quickly glance at her reflection in the mirror to make sure everything was still in place.

When she stepped out of the bathroom, the man was

gone from his table. The door of the restaurant swung back and forth like a broken pendulum and she caught sight of him for a split second—coat slung over his arm, papers clutched to his breast, lunging around the corner—like a streaky photograph of a racing car. Perhaps, he'd gone in search of her. Or perhaps, like her, he was flustered by this moment that had passed between them. That's what this had been—a moment shared by two strangers; a turn in life when something crucial might have happened. It didn't— not out of circumstance but out of choice. It was always important to choose. To know that life didn't happen at you, but was a consequence of everything you did. She could have stayed back and not gone to the restroom. She could have pestered him a little longer, tried to coax out that morsel of life that lay buried beneath the rubble of his miseries. She knew now that she'd gotten up because something inside her said she must leave things alone. For now. Just for now. More chances would come along. As long as there was more to come.

Truth was, she might not have gone with the man. She might have chosen Mark and Maya and the life they would forge together. She could live with that—the fact that she had made a decision. She would be able to accept that and go on and the rest of her life would become all the more bearable for it.

Broadway was a steady stream of headlights. Like balls of fire they appeared out of nowhere and followed all her the way home. The sidewalk drummed under her feet. Above, the sequined black shawl of nightfall. All around her there were people, but being in a crowd made one feel more alone. As she walked, she imagined how she might relay all this to someone; she tried to memorize the evening in a way that might make it easier to explain; later, when things made more sense.

The night doorman was different in Anjali's building but Anita took no notice of him as she pressed the button and waited for the elevator to go up. The apartment was dark. She groped on the wall and found the light switch. The hallway sprung to life like a toy box, objects that had melted into obscurity took their appropriate shape and form. From somewhere came a soft but heady smell of flowers that kept the empty apartment company. The Roman shades billowed gently as she closed the door, then settled back. Nothing else moved, like unfathomable blackness. The walls too were still, which was unusual in New York apartments. It was hard to imagine that anyone lived behind them—the amazing, the unbelievable, the wrenching tales that spun each person's world.

Years from now, this evening would continue to play in Anita's mind, looped over and over, like scenes one remembers from an old movie—grey streets, white tablecloth, sprightly candles, a crisp white shirt with one button undone, brown leather shoes tapping the floor, a stack of dishevelled papers. The conversation and the scenes would often vary. Sometimes they met in Rome, sometimes in Columbus itself, at Le Chateau, where the man would have come on work (he owned a carpet manufacturing business and had a factory near-by). Always they would ride in a car, in silence, and get out in front of a building—doors with arches or grills of wrought iron, and then that long, lighted aisle that led to the elevator.

She would think about it at times more often than others, especially when Maya had grown older and the hours became empty. At first, she would be ashamed of her thoughts, guilty perhaps, that she was betraying Mark in daring to wish for something else. Soon, this would give way to fear—that if she hoped too hard, nothing might ever happen.

Eventually, a time would come when she would dream freely and continuously. The dreams would be vivid and wild. It would take up many hours of her day—many years later, when everything was quite settled and she was old enough to know just how long each story would take.

IV.

LILY AND REECE

Shane liked Reece. They all liked Reece. And Reece's girlfriend Lily, who had a syrupy voice and wore a tiara.

Reece was from Jersey. Shane said he was just a kid and that he'd show him the ropes.

Showing him the ropes meant selling him wholesale. Reece would then make small drops to people's houses—a twenty, a fifty—drops Shane thought were not worth his while when he could just stay behind the bar and have people come to him instead.

"What? for a bag? Two? Fuck that," he'd say and Anjali nodded wisely.

Shane was careful not to introduce him to his supplier, Mr. G, who drove down from Westchester once a month, maybe twice if Shane was having a good streak. Shane kept Mr. G far from everybody.

Reece always wore baggy pants and a floppy collared t-shirt. He walked with a slight swagger, leaning from side to side as though all the baggies he was carrying were tipping him over.

She couldn't remember when he'd walked into the bar, or who had brought him in. He just appeared one fine day.

He was nice to Anjali. Just as everyone was nice to her because she was Shane's girl. She was accustomed to this. In Calcutta, she was always Mr. Ray's daughter to the adults; to the others at school—the girl with the imported stationary and socks from London. The difference being, this privilege she enjoyed. Perhaps because she had chosen it herself.

Reece would come from the back, while she sat on her special seat at the head of the bar, and say, "Where's my dog at?" And Anjali was to reply, "Right here, dog." She couldn't say "I'm fine," or, "good," as was her instinct. She was taught by Reece to say just that—Right here dog.

There was something else in this matchbox room, something beneath all the slight lift of eyebrows, the shuffles in the bathroom, that Calcutta had never been able to offer her. Here, Reece glided easily amongst the turtle-necked poetry crowd and Dan, the other bartender, would tell her of his run-ins with the CIA. Here, no one knew where the other person came from; no one coveted anything special other than a little bump of the pure stuff that Shane carried. That is, other than the professor from Sarah Lawrence, who once lurched forwards to kiss her during, what she thought was an exhilarating conversation about Ibsen's Doll House.

Sometimes, Reece called her Bindi Baby. She didn't take offense. She liked having a special name. Marco was Marco and Dan was Dan—or sometimes Danny. But Shane was

Satan and she was Bindi Baby.

Satan. Or, Shaitan, as they'd say in Bengali. It probably came into Bengali from Urdu which probably came from Arabic, she thought. Once, as they were crossing Bowery, someone screamed. They thought he was a member of a rock band. These little things made him seem even more glorious. Her very own devil. She didn't mind, at least not at first, that Shane didn't care about etymology and was too busy watching *Law & Order* on repeat when not traversing the East Village.

In the months that she'd been coming to the bar, she had never seen another Indian in there. At least, not after the wine-sipping, early-evening, theater crowd had long left. While all the other desis who came for the summer or the ones who drove in on weekends from Jersey spoke of the same velvet lounges in SoHo, the same Indian joints on Lexington, she sat on her special seat and sipped neat Cuervo from a rock glass, watching the baggies slip hands, the re-strained eye contacts.

At first, after Shane gave her that free bottle of Bud, and she started going there on her own, she told herself it was for the poetry readings. It was what any freshman in a big city ought to do. But the little voice in her head knew the real reason. The little voice always knew things you didn't.

In the beginning, Reece didn't bring her around—Lily. Then, she too appeared, one day. Maybe they had just met. Lily was also from Jersey. She was petite, like Anjali, and wore a leopard-print coat that made her look like she had just walked out of those vintage stores on Tenth Street that Anjali often walked past but lacked the courage to enter. A long, skinny cigarette holder would have looked rather grand in Lily's hand, she thought.

Lily had this smile—this wide, thin-lipped, teeth-baring, toothpaste-advertisement sort of smile—that Anjali called the Jennifer smile. Bengalis didn't smile much. And in her family, even less so. Her grandmother, dressed in her white sari, sipping her afternoon tea in the verandah as she waited for her grandchildren to come back from school, would always say, 'What's the need to smile so much?'

'Ooh, I lurve that name,' Lily purred, when they first met. She closed her eyes as she spoke and Anjali could see the thick smear of mascara on her lashes. No one she knew in Calcutta wore mascara. Maybe the air hostesses who showed up at the nightclubs alone. For the others, it would be considered trying too hard.

'From India? Wow. Do you guys ride on elephants?' Lily asked.

To which, Anjali replied, 'No, we're quite modern now. We use flying carpets.'

Lily never stopped smiling. Sometimes, when Reece would say, 'What the fuck did you do with the last bag I gave you?' Or, 'Did I ask you? Then shut the fuck up,' she would still smile like a Jennifer. The whole bar would have heard but Lily smiled her Jennifer smile and soon everyone turned back to what they were doing.

There were other women in the bar: Chris and Jammie;

the Soul Sisters Eva and Jenny, who always came as a pair—Eva as tall as Jenny was short—dressed in black lace and oxidized silver. They typically came on the nights Shane worked and looked at Anjali as though she were nothing but a fleck of pestering lint on their voluminous, synthetic skirts. Anjali had tried to smile at them at first but they looked at her and through her to the wall behind. Now she just watched as they followed Shane to the back and she noted exactly where the tequila touched the etched pattern of her glass at that moment. She knew they weren't buying. She knew what went on in the backroom. But Shane said they were 'clients'. That it was all part of the 'business'. He said this with as much earnestness as her father would when he travelled around the world for meetings. Except here, no one flew First Class anywhere. They hid in dark corners, in bathrooms and backrooms, and shuffled in the back seats of limousines.

Lily didn't talk to the other women. She brushed past them to the middle of the bar, the less preferred part where the riffraff swarmed. She didn't seem to care that no one on that side of the bar had preferred stools. She traipsed in, and even though she was not very tall Anjali could see her tiara shine through the crowd.

She mostly spoke with the other men—her laughter blessing its eternal sweetness upon them as her eyelashes swept the air up and down and the rhinestones on the tiara bounced the glow from the candlelight and shone like a second pair of teeth on top of her head. The men bought her drinks all night, Anjali noticed.

Reece didn't seem to care that she did this. But if she spent too long with any one man, he would come around and intervene in their conversation. And Lily would smile and turn her head back and give him a kiss on his chin and he'd put his hands around her from the back as though this was all part of some secret game they played together.

Reece was always in and out of the bar. Sometimes, he took Lily with him but most of the time she stayed back playing the teeth-and-eyelash game. She didn't check her watch incessantly or stare at the bar phone as Anjali might have done. When he returned, he would head straight for Lily, give her a kiss and slip something into her hand from the back. She would open her little purse without a break in the conversation.

There were times, when Shane hadn't met her eye in over an hour or asked her to come to the back room with him, when she would pass time watching Lily from the other side of the room, wondering who amongst the men hovering alone might offer her a drink. She'd watch Reece with his arms around her waist whisper something into her ears and wonder when her time with Shane would come.

One such night, while waiting for Shane to motion her to the back or come over and give her a little touch on the shoulder—anything really, she wasn't picky—she watched Lily, pressed amongst her men, performing her little dance. And as though she'd known all along, Lily turned around, looked at the far end of the bar where Anjali was sitting, and winked.

Moments afterwards, she walked out of the room and turned right into the hallway, towards the women's bathroom. She smelt of peach as she passed Anjali. Five minutes later, she was followed by a man. In this bar, someone was always following someone or whispering into ears or using the pay phone in the hallway.

It took Lily quite a while to return. Instead of going back where she had been earlier, she took up the stool next to Anjali. 'It wasn't what you think,' she said and looked at her straight. As though daring her to say something.

Then, 'You know, my friend is going to India.'

'Really?' Anjali said, almost immediately, without an appropriate pause.

This was the most they'd ever spoken. 'Where in India?'

Lily thought for a bit. 'Shanghai,' she said.

While Anjali pondered on the appropriate response, Lily leaned forward and said, 'Hey, would you like to come over to my place?'

None of the other women in the bar—the Chrises, Jammies, the Soul Sisters—had ever asked her home. At most, they might say, 'Oh, where's the Satan?' Lily leaned forward and moved aside a stray strand of hair from Anjali's face. Her voice was rough and low, as though she'd drunk a whole bottle of whisky the night before.

'Let's get the hell out of here for a bit. I need to breathe, man,' Lily said.

And, for a moment, Anjali thought perhaps there was someone standing behind her.

They walked east on Fifth and, when they passed the police precinct, Lily stopped and murmured, 'I wonder if Jason is working tonight.'

They went past Avenue A and then B, far more east than Anjali had ever been before. When she'd first arrived in the city, a year ago, she never dared go past First. These days, she went as far as B, which had quite a few bars now, besides Brownies—where one could only enter after one met Brownie in person and got the special handshake.

B, but not C and D. Never that far. And she would never mention such places later when she spoke with Anita.

Anita lived in Massachusetts and was studying psychology. She would have just said, 'Did you do drugs again?' and diminish everything that felt important at that time. As though accomplishments came only from a certain kind of perseverance. Condescension. And that too, from her.

Would Shane have noticed, on a busy Saturday night, that she was not there?

She should have said something before she left but he was too busy and Lily was already waiting by the door with her coat on.

Lily and Reece lived together in a studio in the basement of a grey building on Ninth Street between C and D. It was larger than Anjali's with enough room for a bed as well as a sofa. There was a door at the back that Lily said led out to a small backyard. 'But we don't go out there. We have to share it with the landlord who lives above us.' It was bolted with a heavy padlock and chain.

Lily tossed a black baggie on the coffee table and said, 'Here, why don't you cut us some lines,' as she floated through the studio, picking up this and that.

Anjali recognized the distinct grey-black colour of the baggie and the green stripe on the rim as Shane's. She never carried her own. Anything she did, she always did with Shane. Sometimes, with his friends—the ones she knew wouldn't try to kiss her.

'It tastes different,' she said. It didn't leave her mouth as numb and tingling as Shane's stuff did.

'That's because he cuts it up before selling,' Lily said. She looked at Anjali.

'We all have to pay rent somehow, right?'

What would the other woman think if she knew her own rent came enveloped in a yellow courier package from Calcutta? Call her a princess? She nodded, as though she understood such struggles.

The rest of the studio was bare. There were no plants on the window ledges, nothing. Even during first semester of Freshman year, Anjali had put up a tie-dye bedspread as a wall hanging. Something to warm up the room. That first week, when she was just settling down, her mother had said they should go to Bloomingdales to shop for bedding and, later, she had cut up all the labels on the sheets with a pair of plastic scissors she had to go out to the pharmacy to buy, afraid that the rest of the students, who shopped at the Kmart on Astor Place, would take notice.

'I gotta pee, man,' Lily said, and headed to a very narrow door.

She left the bathroom door wide open, despite the fact that Anjali was present. She wriggled out of her corset and pulled down her black thongs—her vagina was smooth and hairless, like the creamy flesh of a prepubescent girl.

'Do you shave your punene?' She asked, sensing Anjali watch.

Anjali shook her head. She didn't know anyone who did.

'Girl, you gotta shave your punene,' she said. 'Shit, no toilet paper!' She got up and wiped her crotch with a towel.

'Look, no hair,' she said, showing her the towel. 'You feel so clean and so good and you don't smell.' Then, after a few moments, 'Why don't you let me shave yours?'

All the tequila had brewed up courage in her. And then, again, Anjali was too afraid to say 'No.'

As she pulled her underwear down, something warm spread over her pelvis and she sucked in air afraid to let it out as though her stomach, her clothes, her hair—her entire self would collapse if she did. Clumps of black floated in the water as Lily dipped the razor in the sink after each stroke—peeling off the dark tentacles of her past. For a moment she was afraid that the other woman might kiss her. She tried to imagine what it might be like—to suck a woman's mouth, to touch her sprawling nipple. Lily was so close, Anjali could see the individual lines on her glossy red lips. She had a mole near her ear on the left-hand side. The other woman looked up and her mouth expanded, not like Jennifer but demurely. Anjali had seen a postcard in the back room once of a woman in a patent-black corset, thigh-high stilettos, carrying a whip. She had the same look of satisfaction on her blood-red lips. The gaudy smile of netherworld aspiration.

This should have felt like something—anything—but Anjali couldn't feel the sweltery touch of the other woman's hand, of skin upon skin, as she did with Shane.

He never did mention if he liked women to shave their pubic hair, she now realized.

Shane with long black hair and the black vinyl pants and cigarette hanging from his pretty pink lips.

To think Shane existed on this earth while all this time she'd been hanging out with Anita and making small talk with wannabe actresses from The Tisch School who bought ab-flexers from the home-shopping network and watched Seinfeld and Simpsons in the evening.

They say that if you're a Taurean, all your problems start in your stomach. That must be true. Because that day, when she first saw him behind the bar, she felt something deep down inside of her—that somewhere down the line, their lives would converge.

She was nineteen. She'd just arrived in New York for college. She felt free and excited, and she never wanted to bump into a Calcutta auntie in a corner shop having to artfully conceal a pack of cigarettes again. She hadn't cried all the way on the British Airways flight. She knew, the moment she got down at JFK airport, that she would never return.

Home was a place where you could be anyone you wished.

'I want to throw acid on his face,' she'd told Anita afterwards. 'If I can't have him, I don't want anyone else to.'

The city taught her not to be sad. To be angry instead.

She was cold once Lily was done. Cold and naked and oddly infantile. She thought back to when she'd stood like this, with no pubic hair, in front of a nurse when she was nine and had typhoid. Only now, to be hairless down there felt potent not powerless. A few stubbles remained like a scatter of black seeds. The flesh-coloured scar—the remnants of a botched surgical remove of a mole by a gynaecologist back in Calcutta—was now prominent, practically at the centre of her pelvis.

'Here, take another hit,' Lily said, once they were done. Beneath the sweetness of her whisper, were the undertones of resistance, a sort of coaxing command.

This was nice—with Lily—but why did doing drugs without Shane seem so pointless?

When the phone rang, sometime later, Lily jumped up

in reflex.

'Hey,' she answered. After a moment of silence, 'Okay, baby,' and hung up.

She rolled her eyes. 'We better get back.'

This time, as they walked past the precinct, Lily didn't say anything. The cold air slashed into their cheekbones.

Reece was already downstairs. He pulled Lily aside by the elbow. 'Baby, not here on the street,' she said and they both shuffled, untidily, inside. They cut past her with the nonchalance of rush-hour traffic.

Anjali let them reach the top before she went in herself.

She remembered her shaven crotch—the walk back had numbed her in its cold—on seeing Shane. Her vagina itched as the cotton of her underwear—rather flappy compared to Lily's taut thongs—rubbed against her skin. 'Need a fresh one?' he asked. He didn't wait for a reply and poured her another Cuervo. Nothing between them needed to be said. They spoke through his noble silence. In his eyes, she recognized all the miseries of the world. It would be years later that she'd realize it was all nothingness. That they simply had nothing to say.

Lily came back from somewhere through the candlelight. She said she needed to go somewhere. 'Have to make a drop. Want to come?'

It was two drinks later and the tequila had begun to burn. She was sitting on her own, her eyes tracing Shane like a pendulum in a hypnotist's chamber. He still hadn't taken her to the back room. Each time he moved to her side of the bar, to reach for a bottle, she felt now would be the time. The little pinpricks of hope dangling in front of her kept her going all night. She had never really needed the drugs.

'Go with the bitch. Keep an eye on her,' Reece said. Told, rather.

In those short few months, this was the place she'd come to, after she showered, the place she left to go back to her own bed. The place where she too could wear shiny pants and eight-inch platforms and not have Anita ask if she was going to a Halloween party. But no one else in the bar, other than Shane, had ever bought her a drink or asked her over to their apartment. Sometimes, sitting at a distance on one corner of the bar, she felt as though she were a tourist, mesmerized by the glitter of a great city block. But now, he trusted her. Reece with the baggy shirt and loose swagger thought she was one of them.

They hailed a cab outside. There were several going empty at that time, the bridge and tunnel crowd long gone as night ended and twilight began, like a second act. The drunk bum on Second Avenue and Fifth had emptied out his bottle.

'Seventeenth and Third,' Lily told the driver.

'Where are we going?' Anjali asked.

'A party.'

All through the journey Anjali looked straight and said

nothing. As though this was just another thing. She didn't mention to Lily that Shane never took her along when he went for drops or that she never knew what really happened on these occasions. Drops. It sounded so innocent, so pretty—a tinkle of jewellery falling on the floor.

All the questions that begged to be asked. The secrets that remained hidden inside the parenthesis of a city's story.

Somewhere, three oceans away, her mother was ringing for her tea and papers. Her father would have been on his third hole by now.

The drop was at a loft on Park Avenue and Twenty-Second Street—a sort of no-mans-land in her opinion: far too north of her life at the University in the East Village where the nights ran long, where the cheap vinyl stuck to you at seven in the morning like remnants of one's eyeliner. Yet, far too south of midtown where the common folk lived. Where people took trains to places she'd never heard of and stayed in hotels or doorman-buildings with green awnings on polished gold poles. The only area that she knew nearby was Little India, one avenue over and a few streets up. That was where she sometimes bumped into those who happened to be in town from Calcutta—heavily glazed in aftershave—coating their stomachs with greasy curry after a late night out at a Chelsea nightclub. She never knew what to say to them anymore. She'd once told someone—a friend of a friend whose family owned one of the largest hotel chains in India—that she'd like to be a bartender, and he had looked at her as though she'd just said 'prostitute'.

Frankly, these days, she didn't think there was anything wrong with that either.

The loft might have been large but she couldn't see past the bodies that blocked her view. Music throbbed like a hundred heartbeats and under the chirpiness of Christmas lights, she couldn't make out any faces. Once in a while, a voice rose up above all other sounds: Woo hoo.

Or, was it Ooh. Ooh.

A man wearing a lot of hair gel and a tight-fitted shirt approached them. He wore black sneakers that glowed in the dark. Not the sort of person who walked into Shane's bar, most definitely.

'Girl, we've been waiting and waiting,' he said to Lily, who disappeared with him somewhere into the discord of people, leaving Anjali to herself. The room felt mouldy, even at that time of year when everyone else was rearranging their wardrobes with sweaters and coats.

Nothing feels as awkward as being alone in a room full of strangers knowing with all inevitability that you'll never bump into anyone you know. In Calcutta, this had been a privilege—to stand apart from the blow-dried, straight-haired, maroon-lipsticked, tightly dressed congregation. Deliberately, she'd wear two pigtails, thick white liner and torn pants. But why was it that, here, the difference made her feel like a failure?

Eventually, Lily came back, alone, who knew how much later. Everything had stopped moving outside of the shadows and pulses. She had a bottle of beer in her hand which she held out to Anjali, who by then was convinced that her face was marred by the black tear of her eye makeup.

Lily stood with her back to Anjali, bottle in hand, and swayed to the music. For the first time that night, Anjali noticed Lily's shoes—platforms that came up to her thighs, like Julia Roberts's in Pretty Woman. She couldn't remember now what shoes she herself was wearing and didn't dare to look down.

The gel-haired man returned, gyrating his pelvis to Lily's. Then he slid down to his knees, his head at the level of her crotch, as her friend thrust her hips into his face.

'Go, girl, go.'

Anjali wasn't sure if someone had actually said that or if it was a voice in her head—she couldn't differentiate anything from the everything that was all encompassed in that pounding music—breath, footsteps, voices, thoughts— they all became one pulse.

The crowd thinned slightly to reveal an empty plastic table in the middle of the room and Lily clambered on top. Two other men now joined in and she

proceeded to give them a table dance. She didn't seem in the least bit worried that there was any possibility of Reece walking in. She swung an arm up in the air twirling an invisible lasso.

'Go, girl, go.'

Many hours later, and what felt like after many sundowns, when the alcohol had long flushed out, Anjali would remember the night—in the map of her mind—as Lily having taken down her pants while the men licked her vagina, caressing her twelve-year-old punene, as she threw her head back in ecstasy. Drops of beer rained around them. When she pictured this, she could practically feel the moistness of tongue on herself. It made her feel hot and tingling and she was mortified at how easily she was aroused. But then, in the gossamer of the night, she never did know for sure, if any of that had been real or only a hallucination.

When you want something to happen very badly, when you really want to believe in it, it starts to feel true. She often had this dream, and what she remembered most distinctly was the coldness of a naked vagina and the twirling of a lasso. And everything else seemed to slip away—the sound of ambulances outside the window, the bathroom light, the red light on the phone.

All roles she'd longed to play. The other lives she'd never live.

An hour after they'd arrived at the party, they were in another taxi going back to the bar. The lights turned in sequence—green beads a mile long.

'Last call,' she heard Shane say as she entered the bar. He saw her too and set down a fresh, white napkin and an empty rock glass. Had he winked? She couldn't be sure. But the cock of his chin, that must have been real.

Shane didn't ask where she had been but she recognized something in his eyes—a kind of assent. As though, by going out on her own, wherever she had, instead of hovering in that corner all night as she normally would, she had earned herself a new distinction.

Out of nowhere, Reece appeared. He grabbed Lily by the arm. 'But, baby…' she was heard saying as they disappeared into the hallway. The heels of her platforms clipping heavily on the uncarpeted floor as she tried to keep pace.

'Shut up, whore,' he said. She looked at Anjali and smiled as if this was another little love game.

No one looked. Not until they heard the sound. Everyone scurried away from the door and to the far end of the room where the windows hid the daylight. A few, who had had enough to drink, stood up from their seats and went towards the hallway. Shane jumped over the bar. To Anjali, he might just as well have been carrying a sword in his belt. 'He kicked the mirror in, man,' someone said. 'Get your fucking hands off,' Reece was heard saying. 'This is between me and her.'

'Boys, boys…,' Lily said in her sing-song way. A door, perhaps the one to the bathroom, resounded like thunder. 'Stop it, you're hurting him,' she cried.

'Get out, get the fuck out!' That was Shane. She could tell his voice in a concert hall if she had to. The sound of Lily's platforms traipsing down the stairs. 'Baby, baby,' she said. 'Are you okay?' Then all was quiet.

'Is he gone?'

'They both gone, man. Gone for good,' Marco said,

upon returning. He dragged his heavy body behind the bar, poured a clear-coloured liquid from a bottle, and downed the contents of a shot glass like a thirsty warrior.

'I always told yous he was never no good. Nobody listen to me man. Nobody.'

'Eighty-sixed him,' Shane said as he walked back in. He slapped his hands together. His gait as though he were racing a storm. His long hair was still smooth and glistening. Nothing could touch her man, Anjali thought.

When she did finally go out, when she was allowed to, after some time had passed and everyone was sure Reece and Lily were gone, she saw that the glass from the large hallway mirror had disappeared. The frame left hanging on the wall like a giant cork board. Little splinters of glass had sprayed into the room, like foam from the sea.

Shane looked at her and shook his head, as if silently telling her, 'Now is not the time.' But something bonded them together that evening. She too was aware of this. That tonight had somehow been about something else—an initiation. All this time she had been searching and waiting for something to happen, something that would make her her. She hadn't found it back home, in the classes at the University, or while trying to date a budding artist from one of her classes because she knew it would please her parents. This felt like it.

In a city far away, her mother was giving the cook orders, setting the menu for the week. She was probably telling him to make some shukto and ghonto and ilish—the kind of

Bengali food Anjali abhorred. The tequila was warm and almost a little sweet as she cradled it in her mouth.

The bar was a small, dimly lit room with no more than ten little tables and scattered chairs and a long built-in bench along the back. Red walls, red curtains, red posters, red eyes—everything and everyone looked the same. Time had no meaning in there; the only movement of the hours came from the little flecks of light that slipped in through the cracks in the thick curtains.

It must have been well past sunrise. Anjali didn't know for sure. The riffraff had long left. It was only Shane and the other bartender Dan and Marco the bouncer, who stayed last to lock up. She wondered if they would all go to Brownies afterwards. Or, perhaps, Shane would come over to her studio. He did that on nights he was too tired to go out. They sat in a row along the bar, beneath a film of cigarette smoke, as Marco locked the front door and Shane let the alcohol flow freely. The votives had long gone out. The room now lit by the steady slivers wrestling in through the curtains. The empty tables and chairs at the back neatly faced each other in conversation.

Somewhere beneath the music—was it Mazzy Star? Shane's favourite—the bar phone rang, but by the time Shane left the washing-up to answer it it had stopped.

'I bet it's Marquis, man,' said Dan. He had an accent, which Anjali couldn't place, and stretched out the last word till he'd run out of air. Dan had grey hair but the skin on his face was soft and smooth so one could never really figure out his age.

'Remember that one time he came with this girl? I think her name was Sylvie. She was real hot, man. They stood outside and threw stones at the window because we wouldn't open for him. Then the cops came.' He laughed, nervously.

The cops never bothered anyone in the bar, even at six in the morning. But it never occurred to Anjali to wonder why that was so.

The phone rang again, and again it went silent.

'Ignore it,' said Marco. 'I no lettin' anyone else up here now.'

Shane lit a fresh cigarette. He came over and played with Anjali's hair. She tried to act as though it was nothing even though she felt her heart somewhere near her eyebrows.

Then everyone stopped talking all at once and it took Anjali a few moments to realize that the pounding was actually a loud noise coming from downstairs—from the front door. It sounded like a hundred-pound barbell being thrown on the floor.

'I gonna go see who that asshole is, right now,' Marco said, but it took him a few seconds to move.

He came back almost immediately. His breath heavy and his face bejewelled with sweat.

'Yo, man,' he said to Shane. 'You better hide or somethin' man. Reece is here again and he lookin' for you and he says he got a gun.' He panted between words.

It was difficult to remember how, exactly, but Anjali found herself hustled to the back room. To her delight, only with Shane. Dan and Marco were still outside. She'd been waiting for this moment all night.

Shane with the black cowboy hat and the black leather pants and the cigarette hanging from his pretty pink mouth.

She couldn't tell if he was scared. She couldn't read his eyes but she wasn't worried. Nothing bad could happen to her as long as he was by her side.

She sat on his lap and stroked his cheek but he pushed her hand away. 'Not now, baby. Shh. Listen.'

She could hear the voices, boisterous and more than one, but she couldn't tell who it was.

Disinterested, she turned to him again. She tried to laugh the way Lily did with the other men, but he kept his eyes fast on the door and she knew she had to try harder.

'Want to come back to my place?'

Sounds of something heavy being moved around dragged from the outside and then the voices became clearer.

'Where's that fucker? Where is he? I'm going to kill him. I swear I'm going to kill him.'

'Get out of here, man, if you know what's good for you.'

'Who does he think he is? Like he owns the village? Huh? Huh? He can't eighty-six me. Tell him I'm here. Tell him, motherfucker. Right now.' 'Hey, you better watch that now, man.'

That last voice was distinctly Marco.

'Yo, Shane, you there at the back, I know it, you fuckin' asshole. Come out. Let's talk, man to man.'

The sound of glass breaking against glass—like wind chimes. And then a catastrophic noise, as though a truck tyre just burst.

'Fuck,' someone said. And everything became still, as though someone had hit a pause button.

Shane pulled up the window and sat on the ledge, one leg already out on to the terrace which, Anjali could now make out, was on the other side. She'd never noticed it before. Perhaps because the blinds had been down. It was hard to know, in that dark bar, what was closed. The red was all-pervasive.

She stared at the door, waiting for blood to crawl through the crack beneath when the gold knob rattled and Dan's face, also red, appeared. 'It's okay, he ran away as soon as the thing fired.'

Outside, in the main bar, chairs stood scattered, tables overturned. Marco sat in the middle of the room wiping his forehead. There was a large splatter of dark maroon around his feet, which, Anjali couldn't help think looked as though he'd just finished playing with colours during a Holi celebration. He held a stack of paper napkins to his leg. His sweatshirt was black so it looked clean but in-between sentences he gasped for breath.

'I don't know, he must have snapped or something,' Danny's eyes grew like bulging eggs.

'We's told you, dude,' Marco said, agitated and delighted at the same time.

'We's told you that kid was bad news—that first godddamned day, didn't we? Didn't we Danny? See, Danny knows. He knows where it's at…' He paused for air. 'Godfuckin' damn,' he said, touching his leg.

'Fucked up, man. Real fucked up,' Dan said. His words hadn't lost any of its length.

Shane laughed, as though nothing had happened. 'Stupid Jersey kid.'

'It ain't right, man. It ain't right.' Marco shook his head in acquiescence.

Anjali couldn't see his face but the napkin in his hand was no longer white.

'Fucked up man, real fucked up. Hey, you need to go to the hospital, man?'

Dan said.

'Fuck the hospital. Give me some of the good stuff.'

He slammed the empty glass down. 'I thought when he walked outta here earlier, he gone for good.' Marco pressed on the 'g' with determination. 'I thought that. You's told me you's eighty-six him—and I thought fuck, thank God. We don't gotta see his ass no more.' He stopped for air again. 'Now the mirror gone too, though.'

'See, this is what happens when you can't control the women, y'know?' Dan said, pulling that last syllable practically to his forehead. 'You have to have them on a leash, y'know?'

No one looked at her.

'But Jesus, he actually used the gun. I thought maybe it was fake.' Dan shivered, as though clarity had suddenly befallen him like a cold shower. 'I think you should go to the hospital, man,' he said again.

He looked at Anjali who nodded as though she understood everything. She wondered if she should tell Shane she had to go so that he would, hopefully, follow. Everything that night had gone according to plan till this nonsense began. Nonsense. Because it all felt like a game she was privy to watch.

But Shane didn't look like he was ready to leave and she had to stifle a sigh as he set three shot glasses on the table. He took out the special vodka, which was kept in the freezer at the back next to the ice machine and wasn't given out to just anyone.

The three men washed it down in synchrony.

Shane slammed his glass down and knocked the bar with his knuckles.

Twice. He looked at her as he did so.

'Girl, you going home?' And that was when she knew she'd lost the battle.

'I have to take Marco to the hospital.'

'Yes,' she said. 'Yes, I better get home. It's late.'

Shane walked her down and kissed her lightly and she held on to the moistness till she was outside, till Shane locked the front doors again and she turned towards Second Avenue to get a taxi.

It was Sunday morning and the streets were empty. She walked past the corner deli and noticed the glass on its side broken as well—the crack spread in a circular pattern like a spider's web. Did Reese do that too? A bicycle stood below it, chained to a pole. A plastic bag tied to its handle fluttered anxiously.

Everything looked sickly and stale in the austerity of morning's orphaned light.

When she woke up, the phone was blinking red. She hit 'play' and her father's voice came on in a staccato. After all this time, he had still not learned how to talk into an answering machine. In the early days, he'd just say, 'Hello?' and pause, say 'Hello?' again and hang up.

On hearing his voice, her head began to throb gently. Her mouth was dry and her body heavy. She pressed STOP. Was it still Sunday? She turned on the local news to check. She wondered if there'd be anything on the incident but the anchor rattled on about a City Council meeting and some good Samaritan who threw birthday parties for shelter kids.

She dialled her father's number and realized as she did so that he was about to visit that week. He answered promptly on the second ring. He always answered the phone.

'Where would you like to go for dinner on Wednesday? The Spanish restaurant you like?'

'You choose,' she said.

'There's a superb new place in Gramercy,' he said. 'I read about it in the Times.'

'Sure.'

'I'll get the concierge to make a few bookings and then we can decide.' He paused, and then, 'Do you need anything from here?'

'No,' she said. 'I'm fine.' 'How's the money situation?'

'Okay…' she said, in a slightly elevated tone.

'So you'll need more. How much?' and she was relieved she didn't have to explain. She could have told him she had spent a little extra on winter clothes this year and gone out to eat at a few nice restaurants, which meant she was a little short of a month's rent, but he was never interested in knowing details.

Never cared for pettiness. They weren't extravagant—her parents—but provided for her with measured generosity.

'What else is happening?' he asked. Financials dealt with, her father's voice had lost its abrasiveness and soon she relaxed in its stodgy warmth.

'Nothing,' she answered.

'Hmm.'

This was the way between them—the years filled with monosyllabic answers and low grunts, the complacency of a well-aged bliss.

She peeked through the blinds and saw it was dark outside already. The streetlights had all come on.

Did Shane even go home today? She would be able to tell by his slurred speech and the twitches of his mouth. How did people live like that, she wondered—from day to day, with no wives, no day jobs and no bank accounts?

She realized it was probably very early in Calcutta and her father might have been asleep when she had called. But he hadn't complained.

'I'm leaving tomorrow morning your time,' he said. She nodded, although he couldn't see.

'Arriving New York Wednesday afternoon, four p.m. I should be at the hotel no later than five-thirty.'

He waited for her to say something, but she didn't.

'Staying at the Ritz,' he said, although he hadn't needed to. That was where he always stayed anywhere in the world that he travelled to. The relief of undeterred predictability.

Somewhere on Second Avenue rickety tables were being set up again, broken glass swept away.

'Call if you need anything. I'll make sure I answer the

phone. Even though your mother complains if I wake her up.'

'Yes,' she said, 'Yes, I know.'

V.

THE CONVERSATION

nita sat at the table by the corner, the very same table
as the last time when she had come with Mark. That
was six months ago. It was their fifth anniversary and they
had decided to dip into their savings and go all out. They
had even splurged on a babysitter.

It was light outside, the evening brightened by the white
of snow. A car rolled by, a sign of life, that drew to attention
the emptiness of the streets. Behind, she heard the clatter
of plates and cutlery, the low rumble of conversation. It
seemed to her that the entire neighbourhood must be here,
gathered in merriment, warming themselves with wine and
stew.

A waiter came up to ask her again if she wanted anything
else, another glass of wine perhaps, and she said no, she
was fine, her friend would be arriving at any moment. In
between, she worried she might not be able to recognize
Anjali; so much had happened since they'd last met.

Finally, she saw the shadow behind the door—the
exterior door, constructed to proof against the winter. She

knew just from the size and shape and movement of the shadow exactly who it was.

'Hi darling,' Anjali said. 'I'm sorry I'm late.' Her nose was red. So were her cheeks. On her head she wore a fluffy hat. A hat made of soft, white fur that fell over her eyebrows and doubled the width of her face.

'Hi,' Anita said. She attempted to get up but sat back down. She watched, instead, Anjali take off her coat and hang it on the peg, where it draped the wall like a tailored curtain.

Anjali shook off snow from the hat and came to the table. She leaned to one side to give Anita a kiss but was crushed in a tight embrace.

'It was the damned train. It took so long. It was stuck for fifteen minutes somewhere. I don't even know where. Jay something or the other.'

'Jay Street-Metro Tech.'

'Yeah, whatever. Then I had to get out and luckily I saw a cab. I didn't think you got cabs here.'

'It's still the city.'

'I know. I just had no clue yellow cabs came here. That too, on a night like this.'

'We're only thirty minutes away from Manhattan.'

'It took me forty-five to get here. Maybe a bit more.'

'Well it doesn't. It takes thirty. It's still the city. We're still very much in the city and it doesn't take that much time to get here at all.'

Anjali didn't say anything. She looked out of the window. The street glowed orange under the lamps, as though the evening sun had cast its amber rays on white sand. A man and his dog wandered down the centre of the road.

'We love it here,' Anita went on. 'The people are so much nicer. There's a true sense of community. You don't find that in Manhattan.'

'Yes, well, it is rather…serene…'

'We like that. We wanted that. It's nice to raise a family here.'

Anjali reached for the menu. 'Is that the wine list? Let me have a look.' She flipped through the front section and turned it over. Then turned it back again when she realized there was nothing on the reverse side. 'That's it?'

'That's all they have. It's not a fancy wine bar in Manhattan.'

'You don't have to be a fancy wine bar to have decent wine.'

'There is decent wine.'

Anjali studied the menu closely. She wondered if the Malbec would be too heavy and tannic, as some of the cheaper ones tended to get. 'Thanks for coming ahead and getting the table, by the way.'

'That's okay. I told you it wouldn't take long to get a table—forty-five minutes. It's always like that here. They always say an hour, but it's never an hour. It's never more than forty-five minutes.'

'I still don't understand why they don't take reservations.'

'It's just the way they do it here.'

'I know, but I'm just saying…it's quite inconsiderate, expecting people to wait like this.'

'Then you should have gone somewhere else.'

'Where else could we have gone?'

'You didn't have to come all the way here.'

'But I wanted to come here.'

'You didn't have to.'

'But I wanted to. I wanted to see you.' 'Since when?'

'I came, didn't I?'

'Well, this is how things are out here. It's different from Manhattan.'

'I'm not complaining. I just don't understand why they can't take reservations. Who has time on a Tuesday night to wait an hour for a table?'

'We're farther north. We're closer to the city. There's a lot more going on out here. There's some really nice places if you go a few blocks over.'

'I bet they're all cash-only and none take reservations.'

'We', 'we'. She used to hate people who said that. As though marriage made you one. She had to learn to stop saying that now.

'Well, we don't mind. You put your name down and go for a drink around the corner.' There she went again. Would she ever be able to stop?

'They call you on your phone when your table is ready. It's a tradition. People enjoy it. Things are very laid-back here. It's not like in Manhattan. The owners used to personally wait at the tables, but not anymore. Now the woman is too old and can't get around. Her daughter takes care of things.'

'I just think it's stupid.'

'It's not. They're really nice people.'

'Really nice people who are stupid.'

'Okay this is silly. Why are we arguing?'

The last time they had met, things were distinctly more pleasant.

Anjali talked about the fifteen-course dinner she had on the closing night of some restaurant in Southern Spain that served a cup of halibut tea, frogs' leg in a wine glass, a little piece of beef beneath a silver dome of smoke; and who should be sitting near her and had a conversation with her but Sir Simon Rattle.

'Who's Sir Simon Rattle?'

'He's a conductor.'

'What did he do?'

'He conducts the Berlin Philharmonic.'

'Oh.'

A waiter came and stood by their table. He took out a notepad and cleared his throat. Anita had to scoot a little to the left so he wouldn't bump into her shoulder.

'Are you getting a drink?' she asked.

'Yes,' Anjali said. 'I must have something to drink. God, I need it. It's been one long day. I had to go to a really dull birthday party for a co-worker before coming here. There was no alcohol. Can you believe it?'

'I meet friends without drinking.'

'Well, it was quite unbearable. But she's a very dear friend of mine and I couldn't say no. I had to go.'

'So you do go out socially.'

'Not all the time. Sometimes. Only when it's absolutely necessary. She'd have been very upset if I didn't go.'

Anita folded a corner of the menu into a small triangle. 'I guess we're just too far out now.'

'It's not that.'

'We were hoping you'd come for the baby's rice-ceremony.'

'I really wanted to but I was travelling.'

'You're always travelling.'

'I'm here now.'

'But you still haven't seen the baby.'

'I'll see the baby.'

'When?'

'Soon.'

'This weekend? What are you doing this weekend?'

'I can't this weekend.'

'Travelling again?'

'I…yes.'

The waiter, who was still standing there, tapped his pen against the notepad.

'Ladies…?' he said.

'Oh. Yes. Wine. I really need wine. Are you having another glass?'

Anjali asked.

'What?'

'Wine.'

'Oh. No. I've still got half a glass here.'

'Hmm. Hang on, let me see what you have by the glass.'

'Where do you go?' Anita asked. She still remembered the wild parties Anjali sometimes took her to, back in the day. When she had just started seeing Shane. She gathered those memories in a corner of her mind—dark, hidden. Stories she might tell her grandchildren one day.

'What do you mean?'

'Where do you go when you travel?'

'All over.'

'Anywhere interesting?'

'Well, two months ago I was in Paris for a conference.'

She knew there were drugs at those parties, but was always too afraid to have any, even when Anjali offered her some coke once or twice.

'That's nice.'

'Well, I hate going to Paris in the winter. The best time to go is in the spring.'

'Do you go there often?'

'At least once a year.'

'You must know a lot of people there.'

She knew no one at those parties, but the simple privilege of being there was enough to cover that shame.

'A few.'

'That's nice,' Anita said. 'I've met some new people since we moved here too. They all have little babies so we go to the park together and sit for each other sometimes. We're lucky to have that because babysitters are so expensive, you know.'

'So,' Anjali asked, 'How's it feel like to be a mom?'

'It's amazing…I can't put it into words…'

'That's wonderful.'

'Yes.'

'And you're happy?'

'I'm very happy.'

'You look it.'

'Yes. It's hard, but it's so satisfying.'

'And what are you doing these days?'

'I just started a new job at the Department of Health.'

'Oh. That's great news.'

'It's not quite what I want to do, but it's good for now. It has flexible hours and good benefits. Mark quit his job so he can focus on his writing full-time. We need the benefits. What with the baby.' This 'we' she needed for insurance. What else did she have?

Outside, the sound of a store-shutter rattled loudly against the soundless night, the traffic light continued to blink its lonely warning.

Mark must be reading the newest New Yorker right now. They had always read it together and, afterwards, he would share his insightful opinions, teach her new things—a new writer, new ways of understanding a subject; last week, for example, he had taught her a new word. They had discussed the fiction piece, which was a story by someone—a man— she was forgetting the name now. She felt badly, because she remembered Mark admiring the writer. But she could never keep all those names straight.

'Should we get a bottle?' Anjali asked. 'What is it that you're drinking? God! I'd get a headache if I drank that all night. Have something better. You must have something better. Should we get a bottle of the Rioja? Doesn't seem to be much else to choose from.'

'There's plenty to choose from.'

'It all looks a bit…'

'A bit what?'

'I've just never had any of these before.'

'They're good wines. This is a good place. It may not be a trendy Soho restaurant, but it's very good. Few people know of it. But it's better this way. We don't want half the city to land up here. There are lots of places like this around. You just have to know them. They don't advertise.'

'The hidden jewels…'

'Yes. It's the best around here.'

'Well,' Anjali said, looking at the menu, 'I guess I'll just go for a glass for now. A glass of that,' she pointed at the menu and looked up. 'God. Now where did that waiter go? Hello? Excuse me, over here!'

'Sorry, what were you saying earlier?' Anjali asked.

'What was I saying?'

'That Mark quit his job?'

'Oh yes. Mark quit his job and we moved to the studio because we needed to cut down on our expenses. We decided we could do that now, while the baby was still young. We need to do what's important for our future.' Her future now, but she couldn't allow the thought.

'Yes.'

'And this is so important to him.' Anita looked down at the menu. She knew it by heart. She knew that she wanted the cod, which is what she had when she was last there with Mark. But today she just couldn't justify the thirty-dollar price tag.

'Well, that's what makes a good marriage—when one makes sacrifices for the other,' Anjali said.

'They're not sacrifices, really. They're things I truly want to do—for him. For us. It's a choice we've made.'

'And you're happy. That's what's important.'

'Yes, I'm happy.' She bent the corner of the menu back and forth, back and forth, till a crease formed along its edge. 'Yes. I'm really happy. I don't mind this, I know it's just another year. He'd do the same for me.'

'You have a good man in him.'

'Yes. He is. And I'm so thankful that he's in my life and so happy we've made this move. This is the right thing. I feel it.' Her mouth was twitching now and a shiver went up her spine.

'Now where did that waiter go? How long must I wait for a glass of wine? Hello? Hi, excuse me...'

'Just wait. He'll come.' Anita played with the menu till

the edge tore off and she was left with a little piece in her hand. She folded the piece into half, then another half. 'I'd like to go to Paris sometime too,' she said.

'What?'

'A holiday. I really need one.'

'You'll love it.'

'Maybe I'll go next winter, when the baby is a bit older. Maybe Mark will take care of her for a week and I can go on my own.'

'You should.'

'You think so? You think I should go?'

'Why not?'

'How much do you think a ticket will cost?'

'I can't really say. The client pays for me.'

'You think I can get a cheap ticket? You think it's safe for me to go stay at a youth hostel by myself?'

'I'm sure you'll be totally fine. Paris is a very safe place.'

Anita's face lit up. 'I want to buy a pair of shoes when I'm there.'

'You get amazing shoes in Paris.'

'I can't shop a whole lot, but maybe one thing. I can treat myself to one good thing.'

'You should.'

'You think so? You think it's okay that I splurge a little

on myself?'

'You should spoil yourself a bit. You deserve it.'

'Sometimes I miss things.'

'Oh look, there's a waiter. Now if only he'd look this way.'

'Mark thinks I'm too materialistic.'

'It's not being materialistic to treat yourself every now and then.'

'You think so? You think it's okay? Even though it comes out of our savings?'

'Absolutely.'

'Mark wants to go camping and hiking in Colorado. But I'd rather go to Paris.'

No shivers now, but she felt her stomach lurch.

'It's a different kind of fun.'

'I want to go alone.'

'Travelling alone is nice.'

'Yes. I want to go on my own.'

'You should.'

'But I don't know if we can afford it. It's not so easy right now, with Mark not working.'

'But this is just for now.'

'Yes. It's just for now.'

'Things will change.'

'Yes, things will change.'

The room was dark. A single votive flickered on the white linen. The cutlery and plates shone in its reflection. Hot air wafted through from the kitchen.

'This is a charming little place, actually. I'm glad you brought me all the way here.'

'Yes, it's our favourite.'

'Such a pity about their reservation policy because I would have come back otherwise. If I were ever around here, that is. Oh look—a waiter. Hey, excuse me! Hi, over here.'

'Don't shout. He'll come. Relax.'

'They sure know how to keep someone waiting. For a table, for wine. How long does it take for the main course? An hour?'

'You just have to build the wait time into your evening's plans.'

'But an hour?'

'Forty-five minutes. It's never more.'

'But why can't they take reservations? I still don't understand.'

'These are just neighbourhood folk that want to have a decent meal now and then. They don't mind not having reservations. They don't make plans weeks ahead.'

'What's wrong with reservations? The rest of the world takes reservations. People are simply too busy to wait around an hour for a meal in Dyker Heights.'

'Ditmas Park.'

'Whatever.'

'Dyker Heights is much farther down. That's too far. We would never move that far.'

'That is the problem with these restaurants here. They think they can do whatever they like. No reservations. No credit cards. And the worst part is that they can get away with it because the people here have no other choices.'

'Dyker Heights is dull and depressing and far from everything. But it's not like that here. There are a lot of interesting things happening. We love it here. We go to a place on Cortelyou where there's live music on Saturday nights.'

'I suppose it's a different kind of life out here. I suppose once you move here, you don't really care about things like good food and a proper wine list. You can show up in your track pants like that man over there and it's okay.'

'If they took reservations, it would be booked for a whole week in advance.'

'What's wrong with that? At least then I'd know when I was going to eat.'

'People can't plan their lives so far ahead. Things happen. You can't always make plans. You have to be patient and learn to make adjustments in life.' This is what she tells herself these days.

'Well, this is why no one else will really bother coming here. This place will always remain what it is—just a half-decent neighbourhood restaurant. Nice enough, I suppose, but never amazing. Although, why should I care, it's really their loss. It's their problem.'

'It's your problem.'

'Why are you getting so upset? All I said was that I think this is a great restaurant but their reservation policy is completely stupid. Come on. What restaurant in Manhattan would do this? I can think of only a few and they have very good reason to.'

'What good reason?'

'They're good.'

'This place is good.'

'Oh come on. This is just a more grown-up version of Café Mimi—you remember? That little place on Sixth Avenue we used to go to when you came down for spring breaks? We'd get their cappuccino special, which came with two biscottis, because that's all we could afford, and sit in the smoking section? You have to admit, this place is like any old joint in Manhattan.'

'Why don't you just go back to your Manhattan.'

'You're crying. Why are you crying?'

'I'm not crying.'

'Yes, you are. You're crying.'

'I love this place.'

'It's a fine place.'

'It's our favourite.'

'Just with a stupid reservation policy.'

'We're fine with it. We don't mind not having the best. We don't want a front-page review or annoying people from Manhattan making a line out front.'

'But a whole hour.'

'Forty-five minutes.'

'I suppose it's a small sacrifice to make, in the grander scheme of things. Although it's not something I have the luxury to do.'

From the corner of her eye, Anjali saw the waiter cleaning up one of the tables. She raised her hand and this time he saw her. He continued to wipe down the table, picked up the empty glasses and the dirty napkins, deposited them to the kitchen and then made his way to their table all the way at the far-left corner. She asked for a glass of the Chianti. He was just about to turn away when she called him back and said they were ready to order. She got the cod while Anita the mussels.

Outside, the snow fell harder and covered everything, gathering like rolling sand dunes. Anjali worried how she would get home. No taxi would take her in this weather. The trains too might have temporarily stopped running.

Inside, Anita felt that it was summer. Thoughts festered in her like germs in hot dank air.

'It's not a sacrifice, really,' she said, again. Then she scooped out a mussel from its shell and put it in her mouth. It wasn't as good as usual but perhaps, she thought, they were just too busy in the kitchen today.

Afterwards Anjali picked up the tab and they hugged each other goodbye.

She watched while the white-capped taxi disappeared into the snowy breath of nightfall.

It was quiet outside. The calm excruciating.

Mark was babysitting tonight, while she was out. He'd said he needed to get back before ten to finish something he was working on. It wasn't that far to Park Slope, where he was staying at his mother's. He'd said it was easier this way. But Anita had a strong feeling that he'd return before spring. She had already forgotten her name. Anna, yes, that was it.

VI.

NOT QUITE A DISASTER AFTER ALL

The car didn't turn up at the airport. In retrospect, Anjali knew she should have done things differently. In her rush, some details had completely slipped her mind. She had only been thinking of the important things. Or what felt important then, which was never quite the same as what was important afterwards. Perhaps mistakes were better left alone, she thought. Looking back only made everything feel more wrong.

Still, she should have known when she had spoken with Jenny the assistant, a sweet, well-meaning woman who had given her obscure, monosyllabic answers.

'Did you make sure that the florists will be arriving by eleven in the morning and that they know we added calla lilies to the list?'

'Yes.'

'Did you tell the restaurant that the meat will be delivered to them by afternoon and to make sure they serve the chutney on the top and not on the side? Mango, remember? Not tomato. Mango.'

'Yes.'

Anjali had mistaken this for professional briskness. Besides, there were so many other details to oversee— details she couldn't leave up to Susannah, her editor, or the publicist or the assistant, although it was their responsibility to take care of the arrangements. Were it feasible, she would have organized the entire event herself. But it was impossible to oversee everything from across the Atlantic. In the end, she let go of the minor details such as this— the car to pick her up—reasoning, that if it were indeed bungled by ineptitude, at least it would not interfere with the main event. In retrospect, Anjali thought, she shouldn't have agreed to come at all. Things were bound to go wrong and her good intentions would remain buried beneath the rubble of errors.

Tired and annoyed, she wheeled the trolley outside the terminal to the taxi stand. By that time, a long line had already formed. Not a single car was in sight. Abandoned carts stood blocking the pathway and from somewhere in the distance, a voice hollered at her to form a straight line; to get all the way in instead of standing as she was—a little to the side—so that she could get a better view of what was happening out front.

She wasn't ready for all of this, not so soon anyway. She had hoped for a quiet ride with the air conditioner on and the tinted windows rolled up, while her eyes adjusted to the city's glare. Instinctively, Anjali wanted to reply that indeed she was in line; that a deviation of a few inches was hardly breaking the formation; that no matter where she stood, there were still forty people ahead of her and no

taxis in sight and, at this rate, by the time she finally got one, it would be thirty more minutes, by which time she might get stuck in rush hour traffic and possibly be late for her dinner appointment. But the eight-hour journey from London had wiped her out. The last thing she wanted was to get into a verbal combat with a woman who screamed in a pitch proportional to her girth.

Although Anjali had travelled business class and stretched out on the flat-bed as soon as the flight took off, she had barely slept. She had, instead, watched one bad movie after another and managed perhaps two hours of sleep before they descended and was woken abruptly by one of the air hostesses. Someone should have warned her how dreadful American Airlines had become. The air hostesses didn't even bother to be courteous, as if their presence itself was an act of grace.

Ever since she had moved out of America, she had returned only once—to the west coast. She had flown with Virgin Atlantic then. The trip, to Los Angeles, was to meet with a furniture company that wanted her to design their catalogue.

She still remembered how they made her smile five times for the perfect photograph on their visitor's pass. Later, Anjali swore to herself she would never work with American clients again. Constant chirpiness was simply not her nature.

Yet here she was, after all these years she had circled right back to New York. At the very least she should have returned in comfort. Had she paid for this trip she would have certainly chosen Virgin again or perhaps Air France via Paris. Nothing annoyed her more than bad service. It was the worst way to start this trip. Were it not for this big launch, she would have never returned to this godforsaken city, so ugly and so aggressive. She had long forgotten her other life here. Decades ago, it seemed.

The taxis slowly trickled into the stand and the line gradually progressed.

Soon, only half the people in front of her remained, and the group in the middle—there were four of them—looked as if they were travelling together and would need just one car between them. Many of the others were couples. They stood holding hands or minding their children or squinting into maps and pointing. Only a handful, like her, were alone—with a small piece of luggage containing clothes sufficient for just a few days.

Finally, when it was Anjali's turn, she handed the driver her suitcase and shifted uncomfortably to the middle of the seat, her legs wedged in the narrow space, a fact she had forgotten about New York taxis. 'Irving and Seventeenth,' she told him. TALBIR STNGH said the name on his ID. On recognizing her Indian features, he gave a slight nod. She had an inkling of what might follow: he would ask her where she was from and, when she said India, would ask more questions: Where in India? What did she do? Was she married? She looked so young.

Back in the day, when she had lived here long enough that her own accent softened and rolled, she would sometimes say, 'From New York,' but it never fooled them. Not the Indians, not the Pakistanis, nor the Bangladeshis, who were the worst of the lot. Once they found out she was from Calcutta, they would insist on speaking to her in Bengali, ask her where in Calcutta she was from, mention that they too had a relation there. But these intrusions didn't bother her anymore. In fact, she rather missed such conversations in London, where she seldom came across cab drivers from the subcontinent.

The highway stretched wide and flat, as if clouds had come down and turned everything grey. Ahead of her, Anjali could see the traffic start to build. She had forgotten how immense everything was in this country—the cars, the loud voices, the exaggerated dullness of the sky. It felt different now, distanced with the years, but at the same time she had that strange sensation, which only old memories can arouse, a distinct feeling that she was here just yesterday, sitting in a taxi after a flight back from Calcutta.

She felt the beginnings of a mild headache, slight nausea, the usual after- effects of air travel. As was to be expected, they were stuck in the lane that was the slowest to move. She leaned forward and drummed her fingers on the window. She hadn't missed any of this. None of this. She had already made up her mind not to walk past her apartment on the Lower East Side or look for her favourite falafel place in

Greenwich Village. Or Brownies—the afterhours where they all went when the bar finally closed doors at dawn. She actually still remembered her initiation with Brownie himself—apparently some sort of privilege she never quite understood.

Almost fifteen minutes passed and they still hadn't budged. Anjali craned her neck to see what was holding them up. 'Isn't there any other way?' she asked the driver.

He shook his head and gestured in front with his hands. 'Where do I go? I cannot move.'

'Maybe take the next exit?'

He snorted. 'Is all like this. Anywhere you go. Is five o'clock. Bad time now. Everybody want to go. Everywhere is all traffic, traffic.'

She had no choice but to sit back. The traffic became denser. The skyline of Manhattan grew in the distance till a building rose ahead and swallowed them in its shadow. They progressed slowly but through the window everything approached fast and a little too close.

Finally, the driver took the exit for Triborough Bridge and merged on to FDR Drive.

Immediately she leapt forward again. 'Why are you going this way?' 'Too much traffic in Midtown Tunnel.'

'But now we're stuck on the FDR at rush hour. And we're all the way a hundred blocks up.'

He mumbled something inaudible.

'Do you take me for a fool? You think I'm some stupid tourist you can take for a ride? I know New York, okay? I've lived here long enough.' She noticed, with surprise, the hurt tangled in her voice.

The driver muttered something again.

'What did you say?'

'Is fixed meter, no extra charge.'

'So what no extra charge? It's extra time. Then you'll want extra tip.'

She was about to add something else but realized they had begun to move again. Besides, there was no point in arguing. All she really wanted was to get to the hotel, change, make a few calls and check her email before it was time to meet Susannah and the publicist. She decided she would make it an early night. She had to get up first thing in the morning, as there was much to be done. This is what she hated about the city, it brought out the worst in her.

The launch of her latest book—This Good Home by Anjali Ray—was at an Indian restaurant in Tribeca. It was not quite in their publicity budget, but she knew the owners who were proprietors of other establishments in the city and had a long list of faithful clientele—both Indians as well as Indophiles—acquired from the various art shows and openings they frequently hosted. They let her use the space for free and were excited about the prospect of hosting an event for someone of Anjali's repute.

Once the rest of the budget had been fixed, the owners

had assured her publisher that they would take care of all the arrangements. Only, Anjali knew what that meant. If she left it to them, everything would be a disaster. She made a list of the things that were crucial: the meat, the way the spices were to be dry- roasted, the linen and the flowers. After all, the slightest negligence, no matter how small or seemingly insignificant, was still an imperfection. Took a couple of decades, but she knew that now.

It was almost six-thirty when they pulled up in front of an old townhouse that had been renovated and converted into a boutique eight-room hotel. Anjali had found it through a website she always consulted—a guide for discerning travellers—and was keen to see how well it stood up against the high recommendations. To her surprise, it didn't have a proper reception, although the front room, with its wide bay windows overlooking Irving Place, had been converted into an elegant sitting room. There was an old desk (Anjali thought it must be antique) angled in the far corner, behind which, underneath a dimmed floor lamp, was a receptionist—lost behind his papers and directories. Large chain hotels with their grim, heavy curtains, bulky furniture and multitude of guests whenever depressed her. She loved to travel but, she did so, tried to find quainter accommodations—a tasteful B&B, an old, converted church—places with character and charm. She thought of this not as an indulgence but as a necessity, the pleasures of which had much the same effect as a lingering tranquillity after meditation. Crushed plastic wine cups and overturned chairs made her shudder now.

While she checked in, Anjali asked the receptionist about Internet access, not certain the room would provide a dossier of instructions as larger establishments did. She also asked for three plug converters to be sent up to her room—one for her laptop, one for her phone and a third for her chargeable toothbrush. 'As soon as you can, please. I have to leave within the hour.'

The room they had given her, she thought, was good. Not great, but good. The window faced a narrow side street and, if she kept the sheer curtains unopened, looked directly into those of the building across. Nevertheless, this was New York. The only unobstructed view came from the fiftieth floor. Besides, everything else was satisfactory. For three nights she really couldn't complain.

Before Anjali took a bath and changed and tied her hair neatly into a bun, she reached for her laptop. She was sure there would be an email or two from Jenny. In all these months of their dealings, the assistant had yet to figure out how to dial international numbers. Anjali was careful to give out her phone number in other countries with a plus sign in front and omit the zero that was necessary while dialing domestically. But Jenny was a special case.

'I wasn't sure what that "plus" sign was for,' she had said on her first unsuccessful attempt.

'It stands for the code to dial out of your country.'

'Oh,' Jenny said, but from the silence that pursued Anjali deciphered that she had probably never dialed internationally.

'Zero, one, one. That's the international dial-out number in America.' 'Oh.'

'You dial zero-one-one-four-four and then my number. Get it?'

'Yes,' the assistant had replied, but to this day had yet to make that first call.

No matter if something was urgent and needed her immediate attention, Jenny always sent an email.

As Anjali feared, there was one waiting in her inbox. 'Slight problem' said the subject-line. The florist could not supply them with calla lilies. They would have to choose a replacement. She should have known by now that 'yes', in fact, meant, 'I'm not sure' and should have predicted the absence of a car and the unavailability of flowers and who knew what other surprises that lurked ahead.

At least she had made the hotel reservations herself. Otherwise, she might have been stranded with no accommodations, forced to stay at a motel in some remote part of Queens. She made a mental note to bring up the issue of the missing car at dinner. She didn't mean to belittle the woman—girl, rather, because from her inexperience Anjali assumed she might be young—but mistakes ought to be pointed out and corrected so one could learn from them, ensure they never occurred again. It was her responsibility to teach that now.

There were two other unread emails. After the success with her design firm and the two books that followed, she had been, at first, thrilled with consulting requests, the television show that followed. These days, she opened emails with dread.

One of the mails, she saw now, was from a restaurant in Paris that wanted to discuss the possibility of consultation work. She kept that aside, wanting to respond properly when she had had some rest. The second was from her mother. Anjali groaned when she saw the name in bold, black letters on the screen. It didn't matter that her mother lived all the way in Calcutta and that they met once a year. Thanks to modern technology, she followed her daughter wherever she went.

Now that Anjali had entered her forties, people had finally stopped asking her when she would get married. Even the aunts and uncles in Calcutta ceased to bring up the 'M' word, which previously they let drop here and there in conversation, as though it had slipped out of their mouths like a conjunction. But at her old age, Anjali's mother had learned how to use a computer. Every city her daughter visited, she managed to find a son of a friend, or a distant acquaintance, and slipped a mention into her email, carefully hidden between all her other motherly concerns.

Anju,

Wishing you a fantastic launch. Let me know what you finally decide to wear. I still think you should wear those gold earrings with the pearl drops. But either way, I'm sure you'll look lovely. By the way, Navin lives in

New York. He works at Deutsche Bank. You remember him, don't you? He came to your birthday party once dressed as Superman, remember? Call me when you land.

Love, Ma

Anju. She hated that name. Hated the way it sounded. It reminded her of a relative back in Calcutta whom they called Anju Pishi. Anjali didn't know how Anju Pishi was related to them or whose aunt she really was. But the old lady came to visit every other Sunday and, when she did, Anjali was made to go sit in the formal living room downstairs, the one specifically used to receive visitors. The rest of the time, the silk curtains and table ornaments were dusted and shined and the room kept locked, waiting, like a bored and expectant housewife.

As a girl, Anjali was made to chant poems for Anju Pishi, perform little skits to songs and play on the harmonium. Anju Pishi was short and squat and every time she took a sip of her tea, she cleared her throat as if on the verge of making an announcement. When a servant came in offering her a tray of sweets, she politely smiled and refused, saying, 'Oh no, no more of those.' But her mother would insist and push the plate towards her. Then Anju Pishi would refuse again and gently push the plate back. It would remain there, between the two women—on the lace- covered coffee table, next to the teapot and the little doilies crocheted by one of Anjali's aunts. Yet, inexplicably, by the time Anjali was through with her performance, the plate would be empty, all the sweets disappeared, and she would see the little daisies etched at the bottom of her mother's fine china.

Anjali sighed. She was tired. Besides, it wasn't yet dawn in Calcutta so she could wait till morning to reply to the mail. In the past, she had tried to reason but her mother refused to understand. Truth was, she was happy to be single. Happy to get up when she wanted, come home when she wanted, never to have to call anyone to say she was running late, never to have to say, 'I miss you,' or 'I love you,' perfunctory words, which did little to show any genuine feelings.

Over the years, Anjali had tried dating a few times. They were smart, successful, considerate men, but none managed to sustain her interest beyond the second date. Eventually she had given up. These days, the whole idea of dating and being in a relationship made her feel as though she were playing a ridiculous role. From a very young age, ever since she had left Calcutta and moved to New York for university, she had learnt to rely on herself. That, and the fact that she had been so successful in her career, so quickly, meant she would never have to depend on anyone. Even with the mistakes. They were hers. Not forced on her by parental pressure.

She didn't want anything from a man any more—stability, companionship, family—the sort of things her friends did. She knew now that there was no one person with whom she could spend the rest of her life. Her mother thought being alone was a sort of failure. But loneliness came from something empty, whereas her life was full.

For most of the year, Anjali lived in London. Late December or January, she went to Calcutta, when the humidity was low and the winter fog swept across the plains at dawn. In the summer, she took off for a month and travelled in Europe.

These days she didn't choose a specific destination but allowed the holidays to organically form around the beautiful homes she found through a luxury house swap. They were villas in the middle of Tuscany or southern France or by the coastal regions of Spain. She packed two suitcases, locked her flat in Notting Hill and called the cleaning lady to check on it once in a while. The only person she regularly contacted was her mother—every Sunday—relaying the happenings of her week: where she went, what she ate. Her father wasn't interested in such details. If he answered her call, he asked the customary questions and said, 'Hmm, one minute,' and passed the phone to his wife.

It was hard to get hold of her retired parents who travelled often. They took trips with friends to the backwaters of Kerala and spent long weekends in Thailand. When Anjali was younger, she was left in the care of her extended family with whom they lived—aunts, uncles, grandmother, cousins. They were ten children in that house and it never occurred to her, while running around with the others—on the terrace, in the garden, hiding in the secret half-floor by the pantry—that she was an only child. She knew she was lucky. Some people didn't have anything, not even the sense to realize when the one good thing had walked out of their lives.

When her parents returned from their trips, they brought back suitcases full of presents for her: clothes, carefully selected books, shortbread biscuits and vacuum-packed peppered salami. They weren't verbal in showing their affection; in fact, her father never once said, 'I love you.' It was through these offerings that they let her know how much her absence was felt.

She had tried to teach Shane this. She had often told him, 'I don't care how many times you say you love me, you have to learn to show it.' Yet, he always forgot to call, never told her when he was running late. All he gave her in the end were apologies, mumbled in a thoughtless sort of way. His mouth still twitching from the aftereffects of all the baggies he'd snort in all the various bathrooms. The special stuff. The uncut stuff he kept only for himself. And her.

They parted awkward like that too, with token words and an embrace. It frustrated her how he submitted to everything, just as he resigned so easily to her leaving. The least he should have done was get angry. Yet, in all these years he hadn't chased her, hadn't tried to contact her even once. Anjali didn't know where he was or what he was up to and grew slightly annoyed at herself for thinking of him after such a long time. Only at the very beginning had she wondered how he was managing or if he was with someone else. But something about reading her mother's email in New York made her think of him. She glanced at the time. It was a quarter to eight. She remembered she had to be at the restaurant at half past and hoped she would find a taxi quickly.

She arrived no more than ten minutes behind schedule. Someone of her status would have considered this as normal—to keep others waiting—but to Anjali, the slightest delay was an impediment to her routine. She had no time to pause these days. Pausing left room for too much reflection, allowed doubts and uncertainties to creep into one's mind. Whereas perfection was fluid. Perfection was a strong forward motion. It started first thing in the morning when she straightened out her bed and her pillows and kept her yoga mat aligned with the floorboards as she did her daily surya namaskar. A straight mat, her guru had taught her, signified a balanced mind.

When she got to the restaurant, her editor was already at the table, with a young woman whose wine glass, Anjali noted with slight disapproval, was half empty. Susannah left her seat and came around. Her hair was so blonde it looked polished. She pressed Anjali's hand and gave her a kiss. 'You look stunning, as always, even after a seven-hour flight,' she said.

She introduced the other girl as Jenny. 'The publicist is on maternity leave, I'm afraid. But Jenny here has been a wonderful assistant and I'm sure she'll be of great help to you.'

Jenny stood up and extended her hand somewhat shyly, smiled widely to display her radiant dental work and kept tucking her hair behind her ears.

'Now, what can I get you to drink?' Susannah asked. She

articulated her words carefully, with controlled efficiency and deliberateness. This neatness of speech permeated through the rest of her—the grey, crease-free shirt tucked neatly into a black tapered skirt and the red polished toes peeking coyly out of her heels.

'Just water. Thank you. I'm a bit wiped out. I'll have a light soup, see where we are for tomorrow and call it a night, if that's all right.' She was mildly annoyed to find the assistant there instead of the publicist.

The editor turned questioningly to Jenny.

'Oh. Yes, sure,' the girl said. She leaned over, fidgeted with her bag and brought out a large folder. She took a sip of her wine and shuffled through various layers of papers. A few sheets fell on the floor. She picked them up, tried to find their correct order and took another sip of wine.

'So, the calla lilies,' Anjali reminded her.

'Oh yeahh. Yeah. So they can't do it.' She pursed her lips and widened her eyes and turned up her palms as if it were all up to fate now.

'And why not?'

'We didn't give them enough notice.'

'How much notice was that?'

'About a week,' she said, chewing her bottom lip.

Anjali closed her eyes briefly. 'Go for all tulips then.'

Jenny furiously wrote things down.

'Except for the centerpieces. Those will be the mixed arrangements we had talked about.'

'Okay.'

'Can you just repeat what you have written down there?'

'Oh. Sure.' Jenny tucked her hair back once more and traced her finger over the paper. 'I've got hydrangeas, peonies and fruits.'

Anjali waited for her to say something else but the assistant only pursed her lips tighter and nodded her head back and forth, as if she had privilege to a special song, which no one else could hear.

'Meat?' Anjali asked.

'They're good to go. Will be here by noon.'

'Restaurant?'

'Them too. Oh yeah. That reminds me, so ten o' clock tomorrow morning.

'That's when they open. Of course, you don't have to come if you're tired. I'm more than happy to…'

'I'll be there.'

Jenny kept nodding and stared down at her pile of papers, sifting through each one carefully, perhaps trying to locate a missing bullet point. Anjali took a sip of her water. The assistant's face blurred and bloated through the glass. She set it back down without lifting her eyes off the girl. 'My car wasn't at the airport today.'

Jenny looked up. 'Really?'

'Yes. Really.'

'Oh God. I'm so sorry. I had specifically told the hotel. I told them you wanted a town car. I don't know what happened. I'm so, so sorry.'

The glow on Susannah's face, which minutes ago shone like her sunny hair, suddenly eclipsed. The assistant was a new hire, someone she had been fairly confident about and had spoken of with high regard.

'Did you call to confirm?' Anjali asked.

Jenny chewed on her lip and shook her head. 'I didn't think I had to. I was so certain it was all taken care of and…'

'You forgot.'

'No. It's not that…'

'It's not that I mind taking a taxi, you know. I could walk if I really had to. I walk everywhere. But it's just that I was expecting the car, you see.'

'Yeah…' Jenny began.

'It's terribly frustrating when one expects something and it doesn't show up.'

'Yeah.'

'So, it was a mistake,' Anjali said, still not taking her eyes off Jenny.

'I'm sorry,' the girl said, quietly.

'That's quite all right.'

She knew what everyone said behind her back: nagging, petty, monstrous, but Anjali didn't care. Someone had to do the dirty work. People simply didn't have choices in such matters.

'Well, well, let me tell you about the guest list,' Susannah cut in. 'We're expecting quite a turnout. Over a hundred people. Isn't that so, Jenny?'

The editor straightened her chair, took out a pen and ticked off each name as she read them aloud: magazine editors, television people. There would be guests from the Indian High Commission, she said, although that didn't in the least interest Anjali. She had met plenty before. They were rather dull and she usually found it difficult to sustain conversation with them.

'It's going to be fantastic tomorrow,' Susannah said. 'We're all very excited.'

Her editor's enthusiasm had little effect on Anjali. As the evening progressed, it grew all the more abject. Her soup wasn't hot enough and had too much salt and after a few spoonfuls, she pushed it aside and nibbled on some bread, which was not exactly delectable either. To make matters worse, her back began to ache from the sleepless flight. Hopefully, she thought, a night's rest would set it right.

A little over an hour after she had arrived, Anjali was standing outside, about to get into a taxi. She looked at

Jenny who stood awkwardly on the sidewalk, with her arms crossed in front of her and an expression somewhere between a smile and a grimace. 'I'll see you tomorrow. Ten. Sharp.'

There was no traffic at that time of night and they drove down Park Avenue, past high-rise upon high-rise, windows upon windows; the grey pavements sparkled and the city lights squinted in the dark. Each time they passed by one, Anjali saw her reflection rise on the glass in front of her, then gradually recede.

Soon they turned towards Gramercy Park, five minutes away from her hotel.

'Stop here,' she said to the driver and got off on the north side.

It was hardly a park, a plot of well-kept green in the middle of a square. The gates were locked, the residents of the buildings surrounding it being the only ones who had keys. She looked up at the windows, at the little parcels of light, wondering what secrets lay packed inside. Behind each window was a different plot, with different characters. Soon the shades on the windows would come down and the lights would turn off and the buildings disappear, although still standing invisible, like ghostly witnesses to the city's hidden stories.

Anjali walked around the outer circumference of the square. In the dark, the streets were lonely and she felt slightly vulnerable. She had walked home many times like this before with Shane—stumbling over sidewalks. They would be on their way to an afterhours or a friend's house, when the bars had closed at four.

He was tall and Anjali would have to walk quickly to keep up with him. Sometimes, he would stop underneath a shadow that hung from a tree and take out a vial from his pocket. She used to admire him in those days—how he would stealthily hide the straw in his palm, dip it into the vial and inhale in one swift, fluid motion as if he had merely scratched his nose. It was only much later that she noticed the faint tremors of his hands, the twitches of his mouth.

Shane and she must have passed by this park many times—in the summer, when it was full of flowers, or in the middle of winter, when everything was covered with the fresh breath of snow. Back then she never paused to admire what surrounded her. She never cared about such things. There was so little that mattered to her other than what happened behind the drawn red curtains of the bar. The one where she'd first met Shane. From where everything had started, one could say. But there was a thrill in discovering something new, like a new kind of twinkle in the eyes of an old lover.

She had met Shane at a bar adjoining a playhouse where she had gone to see a production (she was learning to appreciate avant-garde theatre from her roommate who was studying to be an actress). He had been working there that night and didn't charge her for the first drink or the second. Afterwards, he had winked and asked her to come back. Anjali still remembered how irresistible he looked behind the bar, in his black vinyl pants that hugged his hips and the fragile netted fabric of his black shirt that shone like reptile skin. His long black hair—cut in a shag, washed and blown—wisped just above his shoulders.

Shane had never been to India. He had shown no interest in going. When they first met, he never asked about her parents: who they were, what they did, where they lived— details one asked immediately in Calcutta—and she was thankful for that. He never asked her what home was like, how often she went back, what the little dot in the middle of women's foreheads meant, whether arranged marriages still existed—questions she grew tired of answering over and over in New York. Never her ambitions, what she wanted to be, why she didn't study business, or medicine or law. He didn't remind her to decide on a major soon, remind her that time was running out, that there comes a point in one's life when you had to grow up.

All Anjali could remember him saying that first time was, 'Girl, you have gorgeous hair.' When she had been visiting the bar for a few weeks, he would say, 'I'd love to comb that hair some day, girl.' Much later, when she had long tired of the cheap wine, the secret meetings inside the women's toilet, the limousine rides to make 'drops', as Shane called the rendezvous with those who wanted to buy from him, it would be, 'I'll be back soon, girl', 'I'm sorry.' He was always sorry then, always came home by the third night, maybe once on the fourth, with his head hung low, expecting her to be home waiting, grovelling for her forgiveness.

And she had, he should remember that. She had always given him another chance.

Shane was several years older than Anjali and rather silent. Like her, he never laughed or cracked jokes or tried to be funny. He preferred not to converse about literature, or art, or history, or drama—all the things she studied and found tedious, and she had taken his disinterest to be that of noble indifference, of one who observed the world in a quiet way. She learnt much later that some people didn't speak simply because they didn't have a whole lot to say. Shane's eyes were sunken in. She could tell by their hardness that he had seen things she never had. Looking into those eyes, she remembered now, she couldn't imagine growing old with him—always perched on the same barstool at the same twilight hour, wearing the same black clothes, nursing the same chilled vodka. But that predictability was warm and comfortable, even in his recklessness, like the moments just before one rose from bed to the uncertainty of a new day, still warm and tangled in the sheets.

At nine-fifteen the following morning, Anjali was dressed—her bun secured with several pins—waiting outside her hotel for a taxi. By nine forty-five she was at the venue in Tribeca. Jenny wasn't there yet, of course. The main dining area was closed off as it was still early, but the lobby door was open and she let herself in. She didn't see anyone. Nothing about the restaurant made it apparent that a major event would be held there later in the evening. But she knew how such things worked. Within an hour the flowers would arrive, the wait staff would appear, the helpers would shuffle about, the tables get dragged around, the manager would shout orders and, soon, piece by piece, the restaurant would transform. This pause was necessary before the night's celebrations—like springtime, which needed the bareness of winter.

She considered waiting in the lobby till someone found her or till Jenny came rushing in. But seeing the sign for the toilets, leading off through a corridor, she decided to make a quick inspection. It was an important detail many overlooked. A filthy bathroom was more than a casual oversight. It was a heinous negligence that reflected on the basic hygiene of a place. Anjali had learned this from her mother, who hated using public toilets—even the ones in five-star hotels where attendants sat by the sink, handing out small towels and wiping the sides dry. Those bathrooms in India had a peculiar odour—a smell of strong cleaning fluid that made their cleanliness all the more dubious.

Nevertheless, this toilet looked well-maintained—with modern sinks and white cubicle doors—four stalls in total. She opened each one to inspect the interior and put up the toilet seats, making sure to hold the rim with tissues. Something happened to women in their forties, she thought in alarm. They all started turning into their mothers.

By the time she went back to the lobby, Jenny had arrived and so had the manager of the restaurant. He wrung his hands together as he told Anjali how he loved her books, that he bought every single one of them, that he always watched her television shows and it was such an honour to host this event for her.

He led them into the main dining area. The walls were painted an innocuous orange-mustard. Or, as Anjali thought, perhaps it was saffron gone terribly wrong. The high-backed chairs were distressed in green and the blue tablecloths trimmed with gold. It was ghastly. The kind of catastrophe that happened when French country met Bollywood.

A swinging door led out from the far end of the room and there was a small bar area in one corner. On one side of the bar were a podium and a microphone, waiting to be set up. On the other, a heap of exposed wires hung from the wall down to the floor and disappeared behind the podium. No bones, Anjali shook her head. The room just had no bones. Everything else was salvageable but it was impossible to work with something that was structurally poor. However, being far west of the city, where space was ample, at least the restaurant was large. Far better than some venues she had worked in, where one couldn't move once all the guests arrived. To think that her apartment in New York had been less than a quarter this size—Shane and she had moved in there shortly after they met. A twelve-by-twelve studio on the Lower East Side, where the bed took up most of the floor space. They ate on it, slept on it, watched movies on it and, if anyone dropped by, all she had to do was stand up and reach for the doorknob.

The manager of the restaurant waved his hands busily as he took Anjali around the room. 'We'll remove all the tables from the middle. We'll keep those small square ones on the side and set up the buffet on the left.'

Anjali nodded thoughtfully. 'You approve, then?'

'Yes, although I have a small suggestion,' she looked at the manager. 'If I may, that is.'

'Of course, madam.' He wore a jacket too big for his thin frame. It hung over his shoulders, halfway down to his knees.

'Why not keep the buffet towards the back, over there, you see? So it is away from view.' She cocked her head to one side and fisted her hand beneath her chin. She liked being methodical. Working from start to finish in a thorough and systematic way. It left little room for errors. Made her feel she was still in control.

'Of course, madam.' He rubbed his hands together, as a child might gesture—with feigned importance.

'And move those wires,' she said, waving her hand at the mass of black cables that left its trail along the wall like a scar.

'Madam, those are for the sound.'

'Put them somewhere else. We can't have them hanging down the wall like that.'

'But there aren't any other outlets.'

'Then just move the goddamned podium.'

The manager looked helplessly around and wrung his hands more furiously.

'Oh fine, just leave it,' Anjali snapped. Perhaps it was only emptiness that drew attention to flaws and in the evening, once the room filled with decorations and guests and music, no one would notice.

'And you know, of course, that the lamb is coming in specially from those butchers in Astoria?'

'Yes, absolutely, madam.' '

And the spices?'

'Madam, just as you said in your emailed instructions.'

'Grind it right before.'

'Not one second earlier,' he said.

When Shane and she had moved into the studio, just months after she had met him, Anjali didn't tell her parents. She told them, instead, that she had found a roommate and that renting an apartment together, instead of university housing, was more cost-effective. She remembered, in the thrill of domesticity, they had recorded their first voicemail together and, in the middle of the night, she had gotten up in alarm at the possibility of her parents calling and listening to the answering machine.

They had debated over the message. She had wanted to keep it short and traditional—briefly stating their names and the number. He had wanted something more indiscreet, a rather long message that went something like: 'You've reached Anjali and Shane. We're kind of busy right now and can't come to the phone. Shane prefers to do it up and down while Anjali likes it side to side. So (there was a purposeful pause here), when we're done brushing our teeth, we'll call you right back.'

He had found it on a website and thought it was funny.

'That's just tacky,' Anjali had said.

'Come on, it's hilarious,' Shane insisted, but soon gave in because he hated to argue.

This win had felt somewhat deflated to Anjali. She was used to sitting around a large dinner table, squabbling with her nine cousins, each raising their voice over the other to be heard. Shane was rather placid. He lacked passion and fierceness, qualities that she was made of. She had told him this once—when they fought one night after he had stayed out too long—that he was weak and easily swayed by others. She had stood before him with her hands folded across her chest and said it was the only thing about him that worried her. 'I know,' he had replied, drawing her between his vinyl-covered knees, the cheap plastic chapped against her skin like his noisy kisses. 'That's why I need you, girl.' It had warmed her then, those sweet words uttered with such sincerity and simplicity in a manner so easy and uncomplicated that clever sentences and dry, restrained humour would only have seemed more effortful.

Before she left, Anjali turned around to take one last look at the room but all she saw were the wires hanging from the middle of the wall. The harder she tried to ignore it, the stronger they drew her attention. Like all the things she'd fought hard to forget-the regulars who came to the bar after the riff-raff had long left; the table dances, standing in front of traffic in the middle of fourth street; the rock glasses of neat Cuervo; and Shane's habit of picking at the crusty residues of white from his nose.

'Don't you have a tapestry or something that we can hang over them?' she asked the manager.

He shook his head.

'A painting of some sort? Can't we paint over them? Do something for God's sake?'

The manager continued to stare at her.

'Well, I know just the thing,' she said after some time. 'We'll put a small table against the wall with a floral arrangement on it. A big arrangement with colourful flowers—orange tulips, perhaps, with a combination of freesias, salal and soft rucus. We can use a long vase and, if the arrangement isn't wide enough, combine two or three together.' Anjali smiled. She loved it when things came together so seamlessly.

She looked for Jenny. 'Call the florists and tell them we need more flowers. Actually, just call them and come get me. I'll speak to them directly.'

'I'm not sure they're open yet, it's not quite eleven,' Jenny said.

'Why don't you give them a call and see?'

'It's still half-past ten. I'm sure they'll be closed.'

Anjali was about to follow the manager into the kitchen, but on Jenny's comment, she turned around. The girl stood gloating, as if she had miraculously produced the flowers out of thin air. At least she had tied her hair in a neat ponytail today and stopped tucking it behind her ears.

For a second, Anjali almost felt sorry for her. She wanted to grab the girl by her shoulders and tell her that everything was okay. People did exactly the opposite of what they meant to do. They always did such things. She should know that by now.

'Mistakes are okay as long as you don't regret them. Regret is for those who don't believe in their own actions.'

'I'm sorry?' Jenny looked confused.

But then Anjali remembered her hair. She had completely forgotten she had a hair appointment at two. 'I said, I think you should give them a call anyway. Ten seems a perfectly reasonable opening hour, don't you think?'

The restaurant kitchen was large and fairly well-kept. Anjali noted some food lying uncovered on the counter and a few scrapings that had fallen on the floor. However, by ordinary standards, it was acceptable. This was hardly a Michelin-starred restaurant, after all.

When Shane and she used to come back home on a Sunday morning, having been out since Friday night, their kitchen floor would always be sticky. It would squeak beneath his feet as he fixed himself a glass of Coca-Cola. She couldn't remember him ever drinking water. The only thing she could picture on his nightstand was a tall tumbler filled two-thirds with ice and soda. She was not accustomed to this habit. In Calcutta, no one served more than a few small cubes, which dissolved quickly in the heat, leaving the drink warm and the fizz to feel rough on the tongue. For this reason, of all the housework she did, filling ice trays was never her priority and she would often watch Shane in the kitchen—cursing loudly at the empty freezer, taking big gulps of soda, belching in satisfaction—with a view of him as rather excessive and vulgar.

The radiator in their apartment leaked as well. When she reached for the blinking phone next to it, Anjali always stepped into a puddle of water. To think she never cleaned it up, allowing it to stay there and evaporate on its own. In the dark, she would fumble for the 'erase' button on the side. She would hold it down without listening to the messages. They were from her parents and she was never in the mood to hear their voice, come up with explanations of her whereabouts, answer questions about her coursework. Shane and she always took a shower together before collapsing into bed, although the sun would be well out. He kept the shades and curtains drawn at all times so the only light came from the two halogen lamps. The television continually ran twenty-four-hour news that looped all day because he couldn't sleep without its steady sound. Their apartment, like their lives, became a cave where time lost all meaning. Anjali couldn't bear the thought of covering windows now. She had specifically chosen her flat in London with eastern exposures so she could wake in the morning with the sun on her face. Her backyard was filled with pots of lavender, rosemary and jasmine, which gave off a heavenly fragrance in the warmer months.

But in that old studio, everything was either broken, or mouldy, or, like the kitchen light, flickered temperamentally. Despite several complaints, no one bothered to fix anything. There was a large hole in the wall, where it had softened from water damage, causing the television Shane had mounted to fall. The bathtub was always wet from water that accumulated when their neighbours took a shower and, one day, she could have sworn there was a tinge of red in it. Anjali could have just as easily asked her parents for more money, a better apartment.

They would have given her anything—the way they gave her jewellery for every birthday and loose cash when they came to New York. But that would involve a lengthy conversation, a plea on their part for her to come home that year. Besides, this had felt necessary, some sort of a struggle that was essential to prove herself and move forward.

From somewhere in the distance, something rang, like an alarm in a dream that never went off. The sound followed Anjali as she wandered out of the kitchen, through a narrow passageway, and found herself back in the main dining area.

Eventually she realized it was coming from her own purse. It was her mother, calling persistently from Calcutta because soon it would be night there.

'Anju,' she shouted on the phone. She always spoke in that manner, as though a higher volume compensated for the distance between them. 'I saw the new episode of your show on the Internet.'

'How did you do that, Ma? It just aired in the UK.'

'Oh, I don't know such things. Mitu came over yesterday and showed it to me on the computer.'

'Oh, I see,' Anjali said drily. Mitu was one of her cousins. Ever since Anjali had started hosting a home-and-lifestyle show on television, Mitu sent her an email every other week, telling her that she should have explained where kantha embroidery originated from, or that the onions and tomatoes in the Recipe of the Week had been undercooked. She thought, by adding her own insights, she was as much an intrinsic part of the show as Anjali was.

'Hmm,' her mother said. The sort of indifference that meant quite the contrary.

'What?'

'Oh, nothing. Just that you were looking a bit black, that's all.'

'It's called being tanned, Ma. I was at a beach all summer.'

'Can't you wear sunblock? It's so bad for your skin.'

'I do.'

'Hmm.'

'What?'

'No. Nothing.'

'Fine. Can I call you later tonight when the launch is over? There's a lot of work to be done here.'

'I sent you his email.'

'Whose?'

'Navin.'

'Wonderful, Ma.'

'He's a banker, you know.'

'Perfect. Now I really must go.'

Bankers, lawyers, doctors. Those were the sort of men her parents still hunted for her, foolishly holding on to the belief that a stable wallet signified lifelong harmony. Perhaps she had been with Shane to spite them. He had wanted to be a photographer, a romantic and noble ambition in Anjali's eyes, although he had never taken any photography courses, or gone to college, saying he didn't have the money.

'What about loans?' Anjali had asked him.

'Who'd give me loans?'

'The bank.'

She had wanted to inspire him, to show him he had so many options, but Shane just grunted.

'They wouldn't give me loans,' he said, although he had never tried, never researched online or enquired at colleges or called banks to ask what sort of interest rates student loans carried and if he qualified for one.

His only asset was an expensive camera that he kept covered in a leather case and buried in his side drawer beneath the spare batteries and broken lighters. He had acquired it as a hand-me-down from a photographer friend. He hoped one day to be able to take classes and earn a degree. He always talked about his first show at a Soho gallery, but that was the closest he'd ever got to realizing this dream.

Anjali had never met any of his family. His father had died when he was still a child and he had been estranged from his mother for many years. She was shocked when he told her this, shrugging as if he'd only misplaced a favourite shirt or CD. 'But she's your mother. Don't you want to see her?'

'We have issues,' he had replied.

The idea of severing ties with her own family had occurred to her now and then. Yet, no matter how many messages she deleted and how many calls she never returned, they were only done with the assurance that more phone calls always followed; blessings for shoshthi and bijoya and other important occasions always relayed; bouquet of roses for her birthday left by the front door (the number of roses always matching her age); annual visits to New York routinely made. Perhaps that was why she didn't mention Shane to anyone back home for the first two years. Something between them had remained disconnected, impermanent. As if she'd always known that this was her other life and one day she would wake up and move on. Yet, it was also this uncertainty that held them together. On days that she stayed at home and cooked for him, laboriously chopping onions and tomatoes, grinding ginger and garlic in a mortar, she felt she gave him something he never had.

In the distance, Jenny's voice called out and Anjali heard the assistant's heels rasp across the floor.

'I called the florist but they said they couldn't do it at such short notice.'

'Then call someone else.'

'Oh, I did. I did. I called three other florists and none picked up. Guess they're all closed on Sundays?' Her hands interlaced, her thumbs seemed to be engaged in a fight with each another.

There was a plate in front of Anjali, a large, porcelain-white serving platter, possibly for passing out the evening's hors d'oeuvres. Her immediate instinct was to pick it up and hurl it at the assistant. But she saw the manager looking at them and checked herself in time. She took a few deep inhalations as her yoga instructor had taught her. Incompetence she was used to—it was everywhere–but it was stupidity that she found intolerable. Although, what did she expect? People didn't fundamentally change. She should know that by now.

'I suppose I'll just have to take care of it myself,' Anjali sighed.

She grabbed her purse from the bar counter and checked for the time. 'I bet the Chelsea Market is open,' she said. 'It still exists, doesn't it? Unless of course you have other ideas. No? No, I didn't think so. Let's hope they can put something together quickly while you wait. Nothing fancy at this point. Yes. You're going to wait there…' Anjali glared at the girl who stood twitching her lips. 'You'll wait till they have everything ready and then you'll put them in a cab and bring them back here, do you understand? Is that simple enough for you to do? You think you can manage to find a cab by yourself without having to call me and say that you're running late because there weren't any free on Ninth Avenue at two in the afternoon or that you accidentally dropped one of the arrangements in front of a bus? Yes? Fine then, let's go.' There was a small part of her that wondered whether taking the subway might be a better idea, but that meant walking a long avenue block to the closest station. She was wearing her kitten heels that day and they would get stuck in the potholes and vents on the sidewalk.

It took the taxi quite some time to reach Chelsea Market although it was on the west side, where they were, just fourteen city blocks north. There was a school race or some such thing that caused a congestion of cars in front. A volunteer traffic conductor held them at an intersection while the last of the runners passed by. It could not have been more than fifteen minutes, although it felt like a good half-hour.

New York was a city in motion—always on the move, propelling everyone forward with its momentum. In Calcutta, where nothing worked, the prevalent traffic jams were just a way of life. But there was something unbearable about pausing in New York—a delayed flight, a dull, drawn-out dinner, a late visitor, a stalled number six train heading downtown when City Hall would close in few hours.

Shane and she had gone to the municipal building in Lower Manhattan on a Friday. Anjali remembered this specifically because she had been paranoid that had they been delayed they would have had to return the following Monday. It was her idea to get married. She had brought it up over dinner one night, when a prospective job at a design firm fell through because they didn't want to sponsor her for a work visa. The first semester of senior year had almost ended. Her parents were already discussing possibilities of her return to Calcutta after the summer.

'This is just bullshit,' she had said to Shane.

'This whole system is bullshit,' he replied, a fact he kept repeating since they had met.

'So then let's just get married. Let's fuck the system. You'll get on my medical plan and I won't have to worry about the whole H-1 visa nonsense.

Marriage schmarriage. What's a document mean when we've been living together for over a year anyway?' She had said this flippantly, as if discussing what to eat for dinner but, secretly, she'd also hoped that he would gradually slip into a role—that he would quit the bar, go back to college and finally think of pursuing a real career.

It hadn't taken much to convince Shane, who never gave much thought to anything—unpaid bills, credit-card debts, monthly savings, the sort of things she now lost sleep over. When they had first met, he didn't even have his own bank account. He would give his roommate his half of the rent in cash, earned from his nightly tips, and go to the post office to get money orders for the electricity bill—the only utility he was responsible for. Later on, when she was much more involved with his 'business', as he called his petty dealings, she'd unfold all the crumpled notes from his pockets. Counting out the night's returns. Always falling short.

They smoked an entire phillie before heading down to City Hall. In honour of the occasion, Shane had bought a cigar from the deli across the street and rolled it with great artistry. It had been raining, the windows were shut, the air thickened to grey, her lungs were heavy as if force-fed smoke and she clung to the railing when going down the subway steps, still wet and slippery. On the train downtown, as it stalled between Bleecker and Spring, Anjali kept singing, 'Mrs Murr-rray. Mrs Ray-Murray. Hurray Mrs Murray.' A woman with a shopping cart stared at her and Shane covered her mouth to keep her from talking.

'Why don't you take my name too? Then we'll both be Mr and Mrs Murray-Ray.'

Afterwards, they went out for dinner—one of the few times she could remember him taking her out. They celebrated with frozen margaritas and blackened catfish at a small restaurant in the East Village. It was a quaint little place, Anjali remembered, decorated with Christmas lights, holding no more than eight tables that were wedged together so close they had to get up and make room for the diners next to them to sit down.

Had they been in Calcutta, their wedding would

have been a three-day affair, under lights and soft music in pavilioned gardens, her body smeared with turmeric on the morning of the wedding, and the day after, at the reception, they would have worn garlands of jasmine and rose—her neck and ears swollen from the weight of gold, hands aching from greeting the hundreds of guests. That was what her mother might have wanted. Her father would have celebrated his own way, in New York, at his favourite restaurant on the Upper East Side. He would have called the sommelier ahead of time to have the red wine decanted and they would have started with a bottle of vintage Dom Perignon. She would have sat away from Shane because couples couldn't be seated beside each other, and from across the table, with subtle gestures, reprimand him for using the wrong fork or laughing too loudly, which he was prone to do after his second drink.

Shane didn't care about such grandness. He was just as happy with potato hash browns from McDonalds. There was one across the street from his bar and he went there first thing at six in the morning, right after his shift. He never read labels on wine bottles or consulted guides for a new restaurant or wished he could afford a holiday in Brazil. Once, in the heat of an argument, she had told him that were it not for him she might have been somewhere in Europe—studying design, history, or travelling the world. 'But you didn't,' he had said, confused. 'You didn't do any of those things, baby.' In Shane's world, there were no aspirations and hence no failures and, in a way, that set him free. Perhaps that's why she had stayed on.

No one knew of their legal union. She didn't even tell her closest friends. To say something would mean to confirm it whereas she preferred this vagueness. Besides, there was something rather exciting about duplicity—when she met with old classmates for a weekend brunch, or with her father on one of his business trips—only she knew the words she had repeated after the judge: love, honour, respect, something like that, a string of meaningless words that felt like a joke but also a secret promise.

'Are you mad at me?' Jenny said.

'What?'

'Just that you haven't said a word since we've been in the cab.'

'I was thinking about those wires and how uncouth they look.'

'I don't think they're really all that bad, you know?' Jenny said. 'It's kind of nice when things aren't so perfect. It shows a certain humanness.'

Anjali could imagine her mother saying the same thing in a slow, thoughtful way as she often did when Anjali was unnerved or anxious about something. From Jenny, however, they were just silly words that hadn't quite come of age. 'My dear,' she said, 'I really don't care what you think, to be honest. I simply can't have those wires hanging about like that in the middle of the wall for everyone to see. What will people say? It's the first thing they'll look at when they enter. I might as well forget to wear underwear.'

In front of them, school children squealed and parents cheered and a little crowd had gathered in the corners of the sidewalk. From somewhere far away, she heard the sirens of a fire truck or perhaps an ambulance. She had forgotten how noisy New York was. She had forgotten its sounds. She used to follow the sounds in the hallway, the sounds out on the streets, till the early hours of morning when the roar of the garbage trucks had faded down the street. Shane had said he would be home from the bar no later than five. But at half past there was no sign of him. An hour and still. At first sporadic, this had soon become a routine. She would call his phone, let it ring and leave messages, skipping dinner, staying up all night wondering whose house he might be making a drop at, staying back for a few lines, a few drinks, a few of whatever else that might be passed along. She didn't know when it turned to daylight outside. Waiting was long and endless. But while waiting, everything else stopped moving.

When they finally arrived at Chelsea Market, Anjali left Jenny to pay the driver, and walked briskly inside. The florist, as she had feared, was of hardly any help. He insisted on flowers and arrangements that were completely inappropriate.

'No, no, no. We need tall arrangements. Tall,' Anjali emphasized with her hands. 'The socket is at least a foot and a half above the table. And the arrangement has to go with the theme of the book, you know?' she said, turning to Jenny. 'Modern, yet eclectic. It has to be simple and tall and wide. Tall. TALL. What is it about TALL that you don't understand?'

When the florist held up pink roses and gerberas, Anjali turned to the assistant and said, 'I can't deal with this anymore. Do me a favour, will you? Go find me a cappuccino.'

'Skimmed milk and no sugar,' she shouted behind the girl, who left in a hurry.

What she really had in mind now was slightly different from her original vision, something similar to an arrangement she had once seen at The Pierre. It was in the main lobby of the hotel, she remembered, which had marble floors and pillars ornamented in gold carvings. Four narrow, clear vases with a single tulip curled inside each one like an embryo. Simple and stylish. The hotel used to employ well-known designers to arrange the displays on a weekly basis. The last she had heard, a big chain had bought it over and the hotel's service had declined significantly.

It was where her parents stayed every time they visited New York, and each time her father would insist on the same park-facing room on the twenty-second floor. From the large, picture windows, one could see the green treetops of Central Park below, like a bouquet in the middle of Manhattan—a coveted view she only caught a glimpse of whenever they were in town. After dinner, her father always gave her a twenty-dollar bill for the taxi back home. He would slip it into her hand, the way one slid bills to doormen and maître d's. But she would pocket the money and take the subway instead. Afterwards, when she called, as they made her, to let them know she had reached home safely, she would say she had been delayed because there weren't any empty taxis on Fifth Avenue.

It was at the Pierre where Shane had met her parents—at the hotel bar, where they had gone for a drink before dinner. It was July, on a weekday, the room was filled with an after-work crowd and below the din of voices one could hear the faint trails of music. With its double-height ceilings and silk roman blinds, there was an air of solemnity and somberness, unlike any bar she frequented with Shane—those that dimmed their lights and lit cheap votive candles to conceal the scratches and stains left on the cracked wooden countertops.

They waited for her parents in a corner, nudged farther away by the bustle of the waiters. Anjali noted what a handsome pair they both made—Shane in his white silk shirt and silver tie and she in a chiffon halter-neck dress, one that she rarely found an opportunity to wear.

Shane squeezed his way into the bar. He asked for a Stoli with orange juice and looked taken aback when told the price. 'Don't worry, I'll use my credit card,' Anjali said and asked for a glass of Prosecco. He looked at her in a funny sort of way, having never seen her drink anything other than tequila.

Shane, who was used to fixing a drink made of three-quarters alcohol, took a sip of the cocktail, shook his head and pushed it away. 'There's no vodka in here.' The bartender held up his jigger. 'It's all measured, sir.'

'Listen, man. I know how to make a drink, okay? I'm a bartender too.' A few heads turned in their direction. Before he could say anything else, Anjali pulled him away.

'Stop it,' she said in a lowered voice.

'What did I do?' He was louder than she would have liked. She often used to think he did that intentionally, knowing how it embarrassed her.

'Shh. Keep it down.' She tugged him by the elbow.

He flinched his arm away from her and, as he did so, some of his drink spilled on the front of his new shirt. 'Shit. Now look what you've done.'

In any other circumstance, she would have said she hadn't done anything, that it was he who had created a scene and didn't know how to behave. But she was aware of where they were, of being observed by others, and at that moment spotted her parents on the other side of the room.

The elderly Rays stood out from the dully suited crowd that in shades of grey looked to Anjali like a flock of pigeons—her father, a stout man, in his tweed coat with leather elbow patches and her mother in a black silk salwar-kurta with a colourful woven shawl draped over the left shoulder. A heavy necklace made of interlinked sterling silver chains and little stones embellished her neck. Anjali remembered that necklace. Her mother had bought it from Paris several years ago. Clutching her bag and pursing her lips together with equal intensity, she manoeuvred through the crowd towards Shane and Anjali, as if silently suffering great pain. Her mother didn't like New York. She often didn't understand people's accents and was easily agitated by the crowded streets. England was more to her liking, a base from where she pivoted all over Europe, exploring cathedrals, palaces, ancient ruins. But that year, the monsoons in Calcutta were late to arrive. In order to avoid the summer heat that still persisted, her parents had extended their holiday and decided to make an unexpected trip to New York.

'Let me get you something to drink,' Shane said, once the preliminary introductions had been made.

As he attempted to elbow his way back to the bar her father pulled him away. 'No, no, no. Don't do that.' Instead, he raised his finger to summon a waiter who brought over the leather-bound menu containing the extensive wine and spirit lists. He put on his reading glasses and nodded thoughtfully as he pondered over the pages. Looking at the waiter, he enquired after their selection of Scotches.

Eventually, he settled for a thirty-year Macallan. Her mother asked for a glass of Amontillado. When the waiter said they didn't keep any sherry, she seemed disappointed and asked for a Campari with club soda instead. 'With a slice of orange on the side,' she said, despondently.

'What are you drinking there?' Her father gestured at Shane's drink.

'Stoli and OJ,' he replied, loudly, although the four of them were standing close together and the music hummed well below their conversation.

'Orange juice,' Anjali explained to her father.

'Aah. I see.' He nodded, as if in deep thought. Food, hotels, books—her father was always particular about everything. In his presence, she would never drink what she did with Shane—cheap tequila that was on half-price during happy hour.

'You know, the best vodka comes from Scandinavia.' In his coarse, Indian accent, her father emphasized strongly on the consonants, rolling the 'd' into a deep 'r'.

'What?' Shane asked.

'The best vodka—it comes from Scandinavia.'

Shane nodded.

'Yes, absolutely the best,' her father went on. 'Their filtration process is vastly superior to commercial vodkas and the taste is so pure that the only way to drink it is neat,' he pursed his lips and gestured with his hands that it was top quality.

'Oh love, just let him enjoy his drink,' her mother said.

Shane continued to smile and nod his head—the way he had when Anjali once tried to discuss Beckett and Ionesco with him, a long while ago, when he had first asked her what she did in her spare time.

'Would you like to try some?' her father asked.

Shane looked at Anjali.

'He's asking if you'd like to try some of that vodka.'

'I think they have a fairly decent selection here,' her father went on.

'Vodka.' He pointed to Shane's hand, when he received no response, speaking slower this time, articulating his words carefully. 'You won't get this kind at a regular bar. It's nothing like that stuff you drink there.' He waved his hand dismissively at Shane's glass. Anjali tried to get Shane's attention in order to encourage him, hoping he too might acquire a sensitive palette one day. But Shane refused to look her way and held firmly to his choice.

When they were outside, walking up Madison Avenue towards the restaurant, Anjali's mother noticed the stain on his shirt. 'Oh dear, you've ruined it.'

'Oh, that's nothing. I just spilled some of my drink, that's all. It'll be fine.' 'You better take care of it, it might leave a permanent mark.'

'Oh don't worry, Mrs Ray. It's just alcohol. It'll come off.'

Her mother shook her head, tragically. 'Tsk. I've always said they fill their glasses far too much over here.' (Although she had never said anything of that sort.) 'How is one meant to get through all those people without spilling?'

'No really, it was just me,' Shane insisted. 'I was a little nervous to meet you, you know? And my hands weren't steady. That's all.' His honesty was charming but at the same time like a child's—one who didn't know how to hold back. He was like that at the very end as well, with tears, and pettiness and, finally, as a last resort, with threats.

Shane didn't get to see her parents again during that trip. They were in the city for three more days during which time Anjali met them alone. They never asked where he was and, later, whenever she spoke to them on the phone, they never enquired after him, as if the encounter had never taken place.

In the end, the decision to leave him had been instinctive, like every other decision she had been able to take in her life, easily and fearlessly. That was how she had done it when she first moved to New York. She had walked straight through to security check at the airport in Calcutta and never looked back, although she knew her mother was standing behind the railing, with all the other relatives, and would remain there till her daughter was well out of view.

That same summer, Anjali had enrolled in a course on Colour Theory at a design school. It was unlike any class she had taken at university, which were uninspiring, tedious, and only a means of accruing credit. But in these seminars she sat in the front row, always raised her hand and passionately discussed colour and space and Fauvism. For the final essay, she planned on writing a paper comparing the post-impressionistic styles of Van Gogh and Cézanne.

Although the deadline was a month away, Anjali was deep in research and would come back after class with new ideas every evening. Van Gogh gave way to Matisse, which led to a study of Expressionism, which evolved into a hybrid essay linking it with classical music. She would return home at ten and sometimes read well into the morning hours when the night had begun to pale and Shane finally came home.

'What's that you're reading?' he had asked once, as he leaned over to kiss her. His breath smelt of vodka, which made her flinch.

'Matisse. He was truly a remarkable man. I mean, you can just tell from his self-portraits the way he…' But before she could explain the green stripes on the artist's face, Shane disappeared into the kitchen.

'Gotta get some soda,' he called out. Their conversation never resumed. Shane went into the shower and when she next turned around, he was asleep, dead to the world. Not even a fire alarm could have woken him.

The week before her paper was due, he didn't come home from the bar again. Anjali was used to his disappearances by then, knowing that if left on his own he would eventually return, like a leashless dog that needed its freedom.

Instead of worrying, as she used to, and calling him incessantly, she spent most of the day at an exhibition at the MoMA—at a show on Abstract Expressionists which her instructor had said they must not miss. When she came home at night, there was still no sign that he had been back. The bedspread and the pillows were smooth, whereas when Shane lay on it, he rarely straightened up and the mattress would remain dented, bearing evidence of his large, six-foot frame. Everything about him was excessive—his broad shoulders, his loud voice, his large pants, his countless cheap shiny shirts that took up more than half the closet, the millions of ice cubes rattling against each other—nothing about him bore any sort of grace.

It would turn out that he didn't come home for the next two days. But Anjali hadn't called the bar that time. She hadn't left messages or phoned every friend of his. When he finally did return, on the fourth night, she was so deep into the final draft of her essay that she had barely heard the door. He whispered he was sorry, and as he leaned forward, head bent in habitual remorse, all she was aware of was the stench of his three-day binge.

There came a time when something good ended and she knew it then—knew that she needed something more, that he would never change, that their bond had faded like smudged eyeliner on a Sunday morning. Besides, she could do it then—pick up and leave with no notice—in a way that it was impossible to take off now, with the consultations and contracts and floral catastrophes. She didn't think of how he would get on if he'd get another job, a loan, a roommate, a divorce.

She just called her father and asked him for a one-way ticket to Calcutta. The day before her flight, Shane came home to find three packed suitcases. That was when she told him she was leaving.

Three suitcases. She left everything else behind, a studio full of useless mementos.

Once back, she didn't discuss him with her parents and they never enquired. They asked, instead, what she wanted to do with her life now and she said that she'd like to finish her degree. Maybe do a master's in graphic design afterwards, in a different country—Sweden, perhaps. She didn't email him or call and when prodded to apply to programmes in America, said she had had enough of the country. She slept on her old bed in Calcutta, in her bedroom still containing remnants of her childhood—stuffed toys, posters, old leaky pens, which her mother never touched in all that time—and never dreamt of the years in New York.

It was much later that she was forced to tell her father about the marriage, when she was sitting in his study one day. He had opened a bottle of rare, vintage sherry and dropped some papers on her lap—the annual wealth-tax form that required her signature. It had already been prepared and filled by someone at his office and, as Anjali read through it, she was surprised by the valuation of her net worth—an impressive figure which, up until then, had been just a notion in her mind. At the bottom, next to the blank line where she had to sign her name, were three options: Sole/daughter/wife of.

Her mother was not in town. It was winter and she was holidaying in Delhi. Her father was sitting in his armchair, smoking a cigar. Something he did when his wife wasn't around.

'You should have told me these things,' he said eventually, taking a deep pull of the Cuban.

Anjali didn't reply. She was overcome by visions of standing in a small- claims court in New York, fighting over jewellery and property she didn't even know she owned; of Shane flying to Calcutta and demanding to be let in as the son of the house.

Her father inhaled a few more times. He saw her remorse. Saw that there was no reason to drag the conversation any longer. The problem with women, he had always maintained, was that they allowed their emotions to get in the way.

'Let's not tell your mother,' he said at last. 'I'll handle it.'

Till this day, Anjali's mother didn't know. The marriage was swiftly and discreetly annulled.

The guests started to arrive by six, those from the consulate being most prompt. At first Susannah stayed by her side, rationing her time, steering her towards each new person who arrived. But soon the room swelled and voices rose over the music of the sarod that played softly in the background.

Pressed for time at the florists, Anjali had eventually settled for one large arrangement made of hypericums, lilies and hyacinths. Unfortunately, it had come up an inch too short. When she strained her eyes, she could see the head of the black plugs just over the flower tops, hovering like a pestering fly. Eventually, another table of suitable height was found. However, being unstable, it wobbled whenever someone accidentally brushed against it, or placed an empty wine glass on its surface. The vase shook ever so slightly with it and, as it did so, Anjali could see the snake-like wires from the sides. All through the evening, she kept glancing over in fear that the vase may topple over.

Soon there was a rush of new arrivals and her editor disappeared, leaving Anjali to get pinned by someone insistent on discussing Spanish saffron. She craved for a glass of wine. It had been some time since a waiter passed by with drinks and she looked around to see if she could find Jenny. She finally spotted the assistant at the back of the room hovering near the buffet table. Anjali adjusted her wrap as she made her way to the girl, intent on giving her one final warning.

For the occasion, she had kept her attire fairly minimal, the only embellishment being the embroidered Benarasi fabric that draped her shoulders. She wore no jewellery other than a thin gold chain with a flower-shaped pendant.

Jenny touched the locket lightly. 'Wow. That's beautiful,' she said, as if they were good friends who discussed clothing and makeup and weight-loss regimes. 'Is that a diamond? It's so cool. You really have an eye for such things. In fact, this whole place looks awesome. I think we've done an awesome job. To think what a crazy…'

Anjali stepped back and adjusted the delicate chain which, on Jenny's touch, had flipped over. 'Shouldn't you check on the bar and the kitchen and see where the drinks are?' she asked. 'And look at those people by the corner. They've got nothing in their hands. Go take care of them.' She shook her head. 'And where's Susannah? I really must find Susannah. It's time for the speeches.'

There were three speeches—first from the proprietor of the restaurant, who spoke so long that by the end whispers were heard rustling through the crowd like a passing breeze; then one by Susannah, who was only marginally better. Finally, it was Anjali's turn and she worried that most of the guests would wander off to the back where the food was laid. She kept the speech short and succinct and, once it was over, sat at a small table by the podium to sign copies of her book. Her throat was dry from talking and there was no glass of water for her. She gestured with her hands at the assistant. Jenny caught her eye but half an hour later the girl was nowhere to be found.

Finally, when the last of the books had been signed, Anjali got the chance to stand up. 'Excuse me,' she said to a passing waiter. 'Where can one find some water around here?'

The man, who appeared to be in a hurry, pointed to the opposite end of the room. 'At the back, ma'am. Where the food is.'

Anjali looked wearily past his finger through the swarm of people and their over-eager smiles. She glanced at the bar next to her. It was empty, other than stacks of trays in one corner and rows of glasses at the back. 'But the bar is just here. Why isn't anyone tending the bar, or is this a free-for-all?'

The displeased waiter tucked his empty tray under his arm and looked around. 'It's just a service bar here, ma'am. The drinks are being passed around.'

"Really? Well, the manager didn't mention this. And, quite honestly, I haven't seen anyone pass anything around here. Frankly, this is unacceptable. Someone should be at the bar at all times in case a guest needs something. Didn't we make that clear?'

'Shane should be here, somewhere,' the waiter muttered. He walked on and Anjali followed. A man was about to approach her, she could tell by the way his body jolted forward. Quickly she turned away and marched behind the waiter.

'Who?'

'Shane.'

'Who's Shane?'

'Shane Murray. He's the bartender.'

They passed by a set of doors leading out of the main room. 'Excuse me a minute,' she said and quickly stepped out. The lobby was almost empty. A few guests were leaving but didn't notice her. A man was on his way to the restroom.

Anjali sat on the settee and checked her face on the mirror across. There were signs of tiredness around her eyes. A few strands of hair had strayed out of her French twist. She pushed them into place.

She slipped back in, unnoticed. Most of the guests had migrated towards the back of the room, leaving the area near the bar and the podium conspicuously empty, like a bald patch. There was still no one at the bar but a corkscrew lay on the counter. She hovered around and took out her phone to see if she had missed any important calls. She toggled through the address book—Alan, Alison, Aman, Asha… She bent down and undid the buckle of her right shoe, which had left a light mark on her ankle, and loosened it. Then followed with the other foot.

When she stood back up he was behind the bar holding several bottles of wine between his fingers. Setting them down, he rubbed his palms on his back pocket to wipe the sweat away and then again on his thighs, in quick, brisk movements. Anjali remembered how she had once sat at the corner seat of the bar, while he worked away through the night—cutting wedges of lime, rearranging the well drinks, standing behind the long, wooden counter with his arms folded across his chest like a bouncer who would properly deal with anyone that dared to cross his domain.

'Shane,' she said, and was surprised at how easy it was to utter the name she'd long forgotten. Something about seeing him behind a bar in New York felt appropriate, as if a normal order of the world had been maintained.

Shane stared at her for a few seconds and then broke into a smile. He came around to where she stood. He leaned to the left and so did she and then both to the right and finally they laughed and gave each other a brief hug, maintaining a distance between their bodies. He smelt of the same stale beer and vodka.

'You work here,' she said, and then silently scolded herself for stating the obvious.

'Yeah, long time now.'

His hair was blonde—which was his original colour but one she had never seen before. Sometimes she saw the roots which he let grow out of laziness. Then she would dye it for him so as not to be forced to look at his multicoloured hair while they made love. It was cropped short now and had thinned in the front. He was wearing a black buttoned-down shirt—those netted, thin shirts he used to wear. It appeared to Anjali as a cheap polyester blend. The colour had faded to a dull grey and, from where she stood, she made out a slight tear on the shoulder seam.

'Still bartending…' Her voice trailed off into a laugh.

'Can't teach an old horse new tricks.'

'Thought you'd be a photographer by now. Maybe had a show or two.' She laughed again. Now she was beginning to sound like Jenny.

He shrugged. 'I got stuff I'm working on.'

Shane picked up the bottles, put them on the back counter and opened the first one—holding it firmly by the neck with his left hand. He twisted the opener around and pulled the cork out in a quick, smooth motion as if he were opening a twist-off. Then he removed the cork and flipped it up in the air, catching it in his left hand.

'Have to work, you know?' He turned around to face her. 'Have to keep paying the rent and the bills and all that,' he went on. He smiled and shrugged again. She could sense his eyes running her up and down. Suddenly, her wrap felt too formal, her hair felt much too done up and she was sure he was laughing at her shoes. He used to make fun of such shoes on other women. He used to call them witch shoes.

He placed the empty wine glasses on a tray.

'This has been okay for me, you know?'

'Married?' Anjali asked and then wished she hadn't. She was so accustomed to being asked the same question in Calcutta—every time she met an elderly relation or an old classmate from school—that it had popped out of her mouth like the weather.

He shook his head. She watched as he poured the wine and one by one the glasses turned to gold, like an hourglass flowing backwards. She was vaguely aware of the faint chatter and footsteps around her, the raag strumming in the background, as if the two of them were far away from the rest of the crowd.

'So,' he said, 'You here for this thing, huh?' he motioned to the crowd behind.

'It's for me, actually,' she said.

'Oh yeah?

Anjali nodded. 'New book.' If she were having this conversation with someone in Calcutta, or Paris, or London, she would have said what the book was about, how the ideas had emerged through her newspaper columns in the weekend edition of Financial Times, which were then compiled into a collection.

'Said it was some famous designer from London or something.' 'That's where I live now.'

He raised his eyebrows. 'Yeah, I know this guy from Paris, you know,' he said, still diligently pouring. 'He saw some of my work. Said they were good and he could use them for a show maybe. You should see some of my stuff. You might like them. I sell them, you know, through my own website. I can have it all mounted and framed, if you like. Ernie down the road gives me a good discount on the framing. I'll throw it in for free for you, though.'

He wiped his shirtsleeve across his face. She wondered if she should ask for a margarita—no one made it quite like him—on the rocks, no triple sec, a splash of orange.

'How long you here for?' he asked.

'I'm leaving the day after.'

'Well, if you got time tomorrow, I'm around. I'm in Bushwick now. It's just a few stops on the L into Brooklyn.'

'That's convenient,' Anjali said. She focussed on the rip of his shirt. A speck of white skin showed through, like an aperture. She had an immense urge to sew it up for him. She was good at things with her hands. She used to mend his broken buttons, iron his shirts, cook Indian dinners for him. She used to spread out the meals on their bed as if it were a dining table—with cutlery and candles and napkins. He must have gone back to nachos and sandwich meat once she had left. That's what he always called it, sandwich meat, no matter if she brought home Genoa salami or Blackforest ham. He looked pale and gaunt. That bar had sucked the life out of him.

'Yeah. It's nice. Big. My roommate is an artist and he has his studio in there.'

'Oh.' She couldn't quite picture him anywhere else other than the apartment they had once shared. It was only there, on the corner of Pitt and Stanton, that he bore any relevance.

'Yeah. It's big. Real big. You don't get places like that in Manhattan these days.'

'No,' she agreed. Perhaps if she had maintained correspondence—a birthday card or a little note like the ones she sometimes sent her mother. Then her mails would have been returned to her and she might have known he had moved.

She glanced back and saw that the room had begun to thin out ever so slightly. The music now rising above the voices, like the sound of waves that grew louder in the evening. She could hear each distinct string of the sarod, counting down the seconds.

'Yeah,' he nodded, still keeping his eyes on the glasses. 'Well, let me know if you want to drop by. I'd like to show you some of the stuff I've done. We could, you know, catch up, maybe.' Every time he moved his arm, the tear on his shoulder rippled.

'That would be nice,' she said with a smile. The sort of smile that came easily to her. She wore it whenever she bumped into an acquaintance at a restaurant, a friend of a friend who wanted to discuss a new idea. 'Interesting concept,' they would say. 'Let's meet next week—coffee, dinner, you tell me.'

At that very moment, Susannah came looking for her. The people from Vogue had just come in, she said, and the diplomats were about to leave.

'Be right there,' Anjali said, and her editor raised her eyebrows as if to say there wasn't much time, and disappeared.

'Hey, Jules,' Shane called out as she was about to turn around. Jules, Julie, My Juliana, that was what he used to call her, and hearing that name after all these years made her blush, as if someone had walked in on her naked.

'You know,' he shifted around uncomfortably. 'You can see them on the website. You can even buy them through there.' He searched through his pants, barely getting his hands into the tight pockets, and wrestled out a card.

'Here, I got one here.' He handed her the creased card. His fingers were dirty and his skin felt like leather. Anjali was slightly taken aback by his friendly demeanour. She would have imagined, given everything, that he might not wish to speak to her. But he was as nonchalant as ever. In all these years since she had gone, Shane could have easily looked her up. Anyone else might have done so over the Internet, might have asked her for things, favours, contacts. He could have reached her through friends, through persistent emails. She knew it was his stubbornness, his pride. But more than that, she knew it was his readiness to accept defeat. The problem was, he never tried, never tried hard enough. But wasn't that what she had loved about him all those years ago—his simplicity?

He pushed the card into her hand. 'In case you ever need, ya know?'

He should have at least bothered to wear decent clothes for the night, she thought. Then again, maybe it happened while he was working. Maybe he bent down to pick up something and the shirt had snared. Maybe he has a nice girlfriend who'll sew it up for him. Maybe she has dinner waiting at home and pesters him to take photography classes. Anjali looked behind her. She spotted Susannah easily, in her all-black outfit and platinum hair. As she walked away from the bar, she looked at the card he'd given to her. Shane Murray, it said. Below that: Parties, Weddings, Bar Mitzvahs, Gigs.

By ten, almost everyone had left and the wine almost gone and only broken bits of lamb and torn pieces of pita and messy bowls of hummus were lying on the buffet table. Anjali was just about to sit down and finish the wine she had been carrying in her hand when Susannah announced they were all heading to a bar on Hudson.

'You are coming, aren't you?' she touched Anjali lightly on the shoulders.

Outside, all the cabs had their lights off. They walked to the closest corner. It was empty. A woman crossed the street. A man slept huddled on the sidewalk, under plastic sheets.

'Just a minute, I've forgotten something. I'll be right there,' Anjali said. She headed back to the restaurant. It looked much like it had earlier in the day—bare, as if the curtains had come down and the set dismantled.

The bar too was empty. Bottles lined the counter and the corkscrew lay prostrate. She knew Shane would come back eventually. Soon, the empty bottles would be put away in the flat boxes lying on the floor, the limes into the refrigerator, the rag left soaking in soapy water.

Opening her wallet, Anjali took out a chequebook. She always carried it, in case of emergencies. She scribbled Shane's name on the top. Below, she made it out for two hundred dollars. Back when they were together, she handled all their accounts. He used to come home every night and pull out crumpled dollar bills from his pocket while she sat with her hands extended. Perhaps he wasn't so irresponsible now. Perhaps it was she who had enabled his dependency.

'Are we ready to go?' Susannah's voice came from the lobby.

'Be a minute,' Anjali said. She pulled the cheque out of the book.

She used to put some of that money aside for their groceries. The remainder she deposited in her bank account to pay for utilities.

'We've got a taxi up front.'

'Coming,' Anjali said. She ripped the cheque into pieces and wrote a new one. For eight hundred dollars this time.

If he ever needed money for anything—clothes, a CD, a junk piece of furniture—he used to have to justify it to her.

She voided the second cheque as well and wrote out a third—for one thousand. Then she scratched out the one and changed it to five. Above, she added her initials to validate the correction. She folded the cheque into two and placed it under the corkscrew so it wouldn't fly away.

'Sorry,' she said when she caught up with the others. 'Just had to take care of one last thing.' She got into one of the two waiting cabs and swept the wrap around her before it caught in the door.

There weren't many cars on the street at that time of night. A strange night with a strange sort of darkness—not the heavy darkness of the countryside, a deep nightfall that made its stillness more pronounced; nor the perpetual twilight one would associate with New York—the kind of darkness that never really arrived and somehow never quite went away. Those nights were rich and full, a fullness that made the darkness turn outwards. Made it complete. But this nightfall, on the lifeless streets of Tribeca, where a lone man stirred on the sidewalk in his bed of plastic sheets and newspapers, was hollow. The sort of darkness that made one feel dull inside. A darkness that gave the only thing that it had to offer—its emptiness.

'They always come out in the warmer weather—these homeless men,' Jenny said, shaking her head. 'When it gets cold, they'll crawl back like dogs to the shelters.'

The taxi swerved right, into an unlit side street casting a shadow inside the car.

'They hate those shelters, you know?' she continued. 'I have a friend who works as a counsellor in one and she said it was worse than death for them. It's not only dirty and crowded but dangerous.'

The cab turned left on Hudson and suddenly the lights came back on again.

'Well, I guess it is welfare, after all,' Jenny babbled on. 'What can they expect? Five-star accommodations?'

They passed by a restaurant with throbbing music.

'The important thing, though, is the existence of such a system, to let them know that if they really wanted, assistance is available.'

The lights twinkled through glass-paneled doors. City lights were comforting, Anjali thought. They reminded you that you were never truly alone.

Susannah turned to her. 'Fantastic evening, wasn't it?'

'Yes,' Anjali replied. 'Yes, it all went off rather well, I must say.'

About the Author

BUKU SARKAR is a writer and photographer whose work has appeared in various magazines and journals including NYRB, n+1, Raleigh Review, Threepenny Review, The New York Times, Huffington Post and Mint Lounge. Her photographs have been exhibited at ICP in New York, Art Basel, Miami, and venues across the US and Europe and she has featured in Fleur and Arbor magazine and The Photographers' Gallery, London. She received the Andrew Nelson Lytle Award for best short story in 2021. Her photobook Photowali Didi was published in 2022. Buku lives in Kolkata and New York. The first screenplay she cowrote, Shameless, premiered at Cannes.